MW00628244

SUNSET AT SKYTYME

AND OTHER UNEXPECTED TALES

Dear bro Jeff,
Keep doing the unexpected!
Have fun!
Brad

BRAD ASHMORE

Copyright © 2019 by Bradley Charles Ashmore

All rights reserved. No part of this book may be reproduced or transmitted in any form or by any means, electronic or mechanical, including photocopying, recording or by any information storage and retrieval system, without written permission from the author. For permissions requests, please address Unexpected Books.

Published 2019 by Unexpected Books
ISBN: 978-0999130315

Cover illustration and design and story illustrations by Steven J. Catizone
Interior design by Megan McCullough

For information:
    UnexpectedBooks.com
      or
    Unexpected Books
    211 Hope St. #4872
    Mountain View, CA 94040
      or
    Brad.Ashmore@UnexpectedBooks.com

This is a work of fiction. Names, characters, businesses, places, events and incidents are either the products of the author's imagination or used in a fictitious manner. Any resemblance to actual persons, living or dead, or actual events is purely coincidental.

CONTENTS

INTRODUCTION

These stories cover a diverse set of themes, making each one "unexpected". There are 4 short stories and 2 novelettes. The genre is science fiction. This is a change from my first book, "Had He Worn a Different Body?", which also included absurd and literary fiction.

Science fiction can be categorized as "soft" or "hard", the latter being more scientifically rigorous. These stories are generally clustered at the center. The novelettes, "Heart of the Ice" and "Venusian Paradise", are set on the Moon and Venus, respectively. They leverage some findings of explorations there, which puts them on the hard side of the center. "Take the Plunge!" and "Kraken Encounter" are in the middle; "Alpha and Omega" and "Sunset at SkyTyme" are on the soft side of the center and rely upon some dreamed up exotic science.

My heartfelt thanks go to those who reviewed the stories and provided feedback: My wife, Leslie, and my children, Anne and Tom. Special thanks to Alex Acks.

Brad Ashmore
July 2019

SUNSET AT SKYTYME

THE SPACE ELEVATOR refracted through the gin flask. The earth anchor skewed through the thick glass at the bottom, tapered into the slender elevator, and distorted into a wavy gray line up the length of the short bottle. The smooth line took an abrupt sideways jump at the current level of the gin. Jim's view of this was rotated 90 degrees as he lay slumped at his desk, inebriated, the side of his head resting on a spread of sales brochures. They proclaimed the many virtues of timeshare ownership in a SkyTyme geosynchronous condominium. When he grew too weary of hearing himself pitch the virtues, the gin stopped the voices echoing in his head—or at least made them less intelligible.

The air conditioning cycled on, blowing chilly air to protect the SkyTyme sales office from Singapore's equatorial tropical mugginess. The sudden cool breeze revived Jim and reminded him that, once again, he'd maybe had one slug too many. He lifted his head, peeled a brochure from his stubbled cheek, and slid the bottle into his back pocket. He ran fingers through his sandy brown hair, slapped his face to restore blood flow, and squinted with bloodshot blue-green eyes out the window at the undistorted space elevator. It was time to brace for the next spate of cold calls.

"Looking good," quipped his boss, whose girth filled the doorway.

How long had the fat jackass been standing there? Who wore starched, white shirts anymore? A surge of adrenaline momentarily cleared Jim's head. DEFCON 1. He took a quick breath and replied, "I find that prospects are friendlier when I am … loose."

"Take your bottle and go. You're done."

Jim focused to keep his wits together. "Sure, okay. I'll leave it at home tomorrow."

The boss replied through a well-rehearsed sneer. "Listen carefully: You're fired." He accentuated the words with angry jabs that wobbled his belly. "I would *never* have you meet a prospect, *never* have you take the elevator and show a unit. I'll find someone to fill that seat who can."

Jim shoved away from his desk and exhaled, hopeless, loose indeed, like a draft horse suddenly unbound. He'd lasted on this job longer than most. Two months?

"*Now!*" brayed the boss. "You've got three days to clear out of housing."

———

It was a short tram ride back to staff housing at the earth anchor complex. As the nearly-empty tram rumbled, Jim watched the cityscape roll by for perhaps the last time. The high-noon sun blazed, which meant no shadows at this latitude. Wherever he gazed, it was just too bright; anything polished was like an arc welding torch. Even the cerulean sky was no relief, as the sun glinted off gleaming faceted spaceplanes. Jim didn't know where he was going to live next, but it would be far from here.

His flat was in the middle of five floors of a dormitory-like residence for space elevator staff, conveniently located at the anchor for ready access. Most shifts worked in the anchor complex, in the elevator itself, or 36,000 kilometers straight up at SkyTyme in geosynch. The dorm was a melting pot of engineers and technical staff, electricians, plumbers, sales idiots like him, and even interior decorators who staged the SkyTyme model homes.

He always used the service elevator because it was fastest, though to press the wrong button might send one to geosynchronous orbit with a shipment. Despite his wooziness, he pushed the right button and moments later stepped out into the third-floor corridor. Boxes on robotic pallets were queued for geosynch deliveries. Threading around these, he proceeded down the hallway that stretched impossibly far. His apartment door unlocked automatically, and he carefully slid in his foot to prevent Flo, his pumpkin-colored cat, from escaping. "Back!" He squeezed in, fending off hyper Flo. The cat turned her affection to Jim, but it was unrequited once Jim turned his affection to his bed. He lay fully clothed, face-down on the cool, rumpled sheets and fell asleep.

It was a fitful nap. He turned onto his back, clothes twisting and binding. The motion alerted Flo that the human was available and so she issued piercing demands. The nearly-empty gin bottle in his back pocket pressed. He prayed for the alcohol haze to mute the rude distractions so he could slip back into a stupor. More than anything, he prayed for a *Get Out Of Jail Free* card to avoid the angry hangover.

The prayers were not answered. Flo paced up his aching body to his face. A vile alchemy of stale fish breath and alcohol-induced dehydration triggered the inevitable. He lurched to the side of the bed where the wastebasket had been, before he moved it yesterday, and ejected the poisons onto the carpet. Relieved, he swiveled out of bed and tossed a sweatshirt onto the newest stain. Alas, he moved too quickly and had to stabilize, hands gripping the sheets, while his head caught up to the rest of his body.

Flo circled at his feet and performed her repertoire.

Jim gathered the lithe beast and cradled her, speaking sweet nothings with his own foul breath. She didn't complain and settled into a position as comfortable as it was contorted, legs askew. Jim tentatively stood, still seasick. The cat surveyed the wider scene and promptly fixed her gaze on an invisible detail. Jim stepped in the direction the cat faced, careful to avoid scattered floor detritus: The sweatshirt, an open potato chip bag, an empty bottle of scotch. Then Flo turned toward something new and Jim pivoted and advanced per the fluffy divining rod. This distracted him from the thundering kettledrum in his head. The sequence repeated, guiding him out of the bedroom and through his apartment along a mysterious chain of waypoints. Jim took direction well—when it was in the direction he was willing to go, anyway.

A fly zoomed past and snagged Flo's attention. Jim swerved her in pursuit of the prey, which drew the duo into WWI-style aerial combat, a cat dogfight. Her fuzzy arms flailed like a frenetic orchestra conductor. Alas, Jim was hopelessly slow and the fly easily outmaneuvered them. In obvious disappointment, Flo demanded to be put down.

Jim managed to fill Flo's kibble bowl and then sunk to the kitchen floor to sit against the cool wall. To keep his head from exploding he squeezed his eyes shut, but that only conjured memories of the asinine scenario that had ended here on the floor: Not the cat and the fly, but his equally aimless life. Fired from another job. Now it was time to revisit the job boards. Networking was out of the question with a social landscape scarred by burned bridges. Why did some people have a calling, an almost instinctive drive to follow a path to fulfillment? Why not him? He was like a mouse in a maze, a maze with an electric shock at each wrong turn. Each time he was fired from a job there was a jolt. Hence, the booze to get past the pain, to mute the insecurity of aimlessness. He didn't even know what the "cheese" was at the end. The lucky people knew.

As he sat and reassembled himself, the cat crunched her kibble and the fly parked in a sunbeam on the grimy countertop. Its silvery wings opened to catch the rays. At the rear tip of its body, a tiny blue light blinked.

After several minutes in the sun, the fly went aloft. It hovered over Flo and Jim, tracing a lazy figure eight which tantalized the cat. "Crap." Jim opened his eyes, stood, and grabbed a newspaper with one hand while leaning on the counter for support.

Flo paced back and forth under the fly as Jim took a mighty swing, which the fly easily dodged. It flew to the closed door, zooming chaotically and deftly avoiding volleys of newspaper blows. The cat tracked and feline-narrated the fly's every move. Then Jim got the bright idea to open the door to let the fly out of the apartment.

Thus began perhaps the highlight of Flo's life, as she bounded after the fly and Jim staggered after her, desperately wishing he were still in bed. "Damn it, Flo!" echoed down the infinite hallway. The caravan zig-zagged toward the service elevator, where the fly alighted on the ceiling over a large corrugated cardboard box on a pallet. Flo circled the box, chattering. Then, as Jim neared, the fly descended to the side of the box and crawled under the lid. Flo raced to sink her claws into cardboard and pulled herself up. Before Jim could intervene, Flo had squeezed under the lid and into the box as well. Now it was "Shit!" that his neighbors heard.

Jim was able to flip off the lid and, in his exhaustion, saw the Holy Grail: A new couch. The fly had ducked underneath the couch and Flo strained to reach it. But Jim had seen enough. He clambered in, collapsed on the couch, and declared, as he often did on his random walk through life: "I'll sort this out later." He was asleep in seconds.

Nearly comatose, Jim was unaware as the robotic pallet activated and rolled into the elevator. He was equally unaware of the high acceleration that pressed him into the couch as the elevator ascended to the couch's destination, a SkyTyme model condominium. Flo was also pinned to the couch, but the steady pressure had the calming effect of a heavy blanket on her. She slept, curled next to Jim.

After a few hours of freight-worthy acceleration and deceleration, the box arrived at the SkyTyme robotic shipping depot from which it was a short roll to the partially-staged condominium.

Upon arrival inside the condominium, the robotic pallet beeped loudly to summon a recipient, but the model home was empty. The alert awoke Jim with a start. His sudden movement propelled him off the couch, against the side of the box, then gently back down to the couch. "Shit!" was heard by nobody. Jim was vividly aware of the situation. Being 98% weightless meant he was far from home and it would be a long time before he had a good night's sleep. Flo opened her eyes and then closed them; no news was good news. A steady humming sound, like a fan or compressor, could be heard from the room.

Jim sighed and gave a shove to propel himself out of the open box. He drifted toward the high, padded ceiling and saw the source of the humming below: A dense swarm of thousands of silvery flies in the middle of the room. A misplaced push off the ceiling cast him tumbling toward the swarm, flailing uselessly. The flies quickly pulled back into a sphere that floated to the side. As he collided with the floor, he gripped the carpet, then steadied himself as he carefully stood.

He examined the flies. They were the same as the one in his apartment and, he realized on now more sober reflection, unlike any he had ever seen before. They had polished, silvery bodies and, if his eyes weren't fooling him, the occasional flash of saturated red, blue, and green light. They were almost beautiful… almost.

Jim felt his back pocket and pulled out the flask, which fortunately held enough for one last good gulp. This situation called for steady nerves.

The last belt of gin burned its way down as Jim grimaced. The spherical fly cloud changed shape into a torus that whirred around his head. Sunlight glinted off the mirrored, flickering bodies. As the alcohol's warmth percolated to his extremities, a hypnotic fog descended. The bottle slipped out of his relaxed hand and slowly coasted toward the floor.

The torus diffused and the flies rearranged into a tight square grid in front of Jim's glazed eyes; their tiny tail lights glowed like pixels.

As he stared, mesmerized, a thick, red ring was rendered across the floating, silver-gray matrix. The ring shrank, another large one took its place, and another, and more. The retreating concentric rings drew him in until the flies' hold on Jim was complete.

The hypnotic circles dissolved into an astronomical scene of the earth, with elevator, and the sun. A scatter of nearby stars was visible. One of these blinked.

Rings radiated from the earth and, as if the planet sent ripples across an interstellar pond, the widening ripples passed local stars and encountered the blinking star. The view centered on that star and zoomed in to center on an orbiting green planet. The planet grew larger until surface features were apparent: Dull blue-green land masses and glossy yellow-green seas under lacy gray-green clouds.

On the night side of the planet, brilliant points of blue light clustered in what appeared to be cities, strung together by wispy blue tendrils. The image centered on a city cluster and zoomed in to show ground-level detail with a towering forest in the midst of glowing blue rectilinear structures. The earth ripples swept across the forest and agitated the trees. They bent and the gracile branches seemed to reach and grab at the ripples. The forest swayed in harmony with the interstellar signal.

The next animated scene showed the outline of a silver fly. A chain of square waves scrolled from its head to a flickering multi-colored tail light. The outline filled in with silver and the scene zoomed out to show the fly surrounded by countless other silver flies arranged in a solid circle. Their wings opened in unison and interconnected, filling the space between them to make a great, polished silver disk.

Against the original astronomical scene, the disk floated next to the green planet. Cascading ripples from the earth continued. Dotted lines from the green planet streamed toward the disk, and, as if pushed by dotted line pulses, the disk accelerated toward the earth.

The pulses stopped and the disk coasted across the astronomical scene, past the local stars, toward the earth. A shower of fine white dots from our sun slowed the disk. The earth was not on the disk's path, so the disk pivoted to use the sun shower to change tack to intercept the elevator that swung three Earth diameters into space. This ended the disk's journey.

The next scenes of this spectacle began with the flies in SkyTyme, depicted as a green circle, tied to the earth by the elevator. The earth's radiating ripples emanated from the center of the planet. Fly scouts descended the elevator to apparently seek the source of the ripples. Each scout returned to SkyTyme to be replaced by another.

At last, a fly reached the source. In a flash, the image changed to a high resolution closeup of spastic Flo held by bleary-eyed Jim. This climactic view from the fly in Jim's apartment showed that, at last, someone had taken the bait.

Jim exhaled, unaware he had been holding his breath. He gasped at the image of Flo's giant orange head, gaping mouth baring pointy teeth. He raised his arms to brush it away, but balked. The flies' subliminal message bubbled up from his subconscious. Realization crystallized, lifting the last of the alcoholic fog.

"Flo! My apartment! What the heck!"

The flies maintained the floating image, hovering with little effort in low G while Jim calmed.

"OK, whatever you are: What's next? Why me?"

Jim's reaction seemed to cue the flies to render the final and most important scenes of their montage. Only now Jim was fully aware, a clear-headed student intent on learning.

A cartoony stick figure, presumably Jim, stood next to a rectangle flickering with animation, the fly array. The array rearranged to form a circle that surrounded stick figure Jim. The circle shrank, erasing Jim as it did until the array was a solid dot with no trace of Jim.

The next scene was a shallow parabola with the dot at its focal point. The dot showered tiny specks towards the parabola. These reflected in a collimated beam until the dot evaporated, as if it had been beamed away.

The original astronomical scene returned, now with the beam from the elevator. The beam traversed the nearby stars toward the forested planet, where a receiving parabola waited.

The receiving parabola filled the screen and the dot reassembled from the captured beam. Amidst the swaying forest entities and iridescent blue rectangles, the dot expanded into a circle, a circle that revealed stick figure Jim.

In the final scene, the stick figure moved its arms and legs, like jumping jacks, looking as healthy as a stick figure could. In unison, the trees mimicked the motion, in their ungainly way. This repeated several times and then the image faded to the neutral color of the silver-gray fly matrix.

Jim wiped away tears that pooled on his face. Opportunity was revealed as if through an open door that had been forever closed. "A way out of the maze".

If he hadn't been facing away from the window, he would have seen the sun setting 36,000 kilometers and a horizon away. The last sunlight splashed onto the far wall in a trapezoidal shape cut by the window. The flies migrated to the sunlight and spread to fit the shape, opening their wings. But the patch of light was too small for all of them. They circulated, so the flies on top would soak up sunlight and then burrow into the stack of silver bodies as others writhed their way into the light.

As he watched the swarm, he struggled with the prospect of leaping from failed timeshare salesman to interstellar ambassador. Jim turned to the window and noticed that with a simple pull, a shade would block all of the light. Turning back, he watched the flies in their solar feeding frenzy. He could starve them all; he was in control. But that pull would also commit him to the electrified maze and the booze.

Beneath the shimmering trapezoid waited a wet bar stocked with bottles of spirits. His future was in his hands. What he wouldn't give for a drink and here was a whole bar. He glided over to the bar under the patch of humming flies. A bottle of scotch was front and center. With a twist of the cap and a gulp, he gagged and spat it out.

"Tea! Son of a bitch! It's tea!" In that moment, he loathed the interior decorators even more than his former boss.

The trapezoid had trimmed into a slender triangle that was disappearing before his eyes as the flies churned. He threw the bottle of staged scotch down to the floor. It bounced and spun; tea fanned out into the room. "Shit."

The sunlight disappeared and the flies, sufficiently recharged, migrated into the center of the room. They formed a shiny parabola that spanned the height of the room. Jim knew where it was aimed. Then he peeked into the open freight box and saw Flo asleep, curled up on the couch. On the other side of the box was the service delivery port. He could retrace his path back to… where? After he cleared out his apartment, what was next? It was down to the life he knew and hated or the extraordinary unknown. Which did he fear most: Zero or infinity?

A couple of flies dropped to the carpet, out of power. They seemed to lose shape and melt.

He glanced back at the box to tell sleeping Flo, "You stay here. Stay safe… stay silly." After a couple of deep breaths, he stepped to the focal point, turned to face the afterglow of sunset below, and waited.

The buzzing grew louder, and flies swarmed around him with such velocity that they blurred his view of the earth until everything was dark. The buzzing faded away and he felt completely weightless, formless, and detached from the flies, the room, and reality.

The buzzing returned, but in a different key. As though awakened from a short nap, he felt refreshed. He was conscious of his strong heartbeat. He was conscious of something else, too, something cool and rubbery that stroked his arm.

Back in the SkyTyme condo, the interior decorator arrived to finish up. She opened the door and screamed as an orange cat sailed out. There was a metallic, burnt smell and in the center of the room spread a gray puddle. Looking about, she saw that clearly someone or something (the cat?) had disturbed the faux wet bar and the freight shipment.

Many light years away, Jim was learning how to interact with his new planetary family, as eager as they were to discover everything there was to discover.

TAKE THE PLUNGE!

MY ExWHY POD vibrated. I yanked it from my pocket to be notified that Ellen and Jerry were about to stop by from their dinner date, that almond milk was better for me than dairy and so it had placed an order, and that the time had come to give scuba diving another try so travel had been arranged to the Bahamas.

I squirmed on the couch, fretting about the scuba trip. I had never considered scuba diving before ExWhy signed me up for lessons months ago. Those went well enough, I suppose, but they were in a local swimming pool. The showstopper came later: The open ocean dive. When the time came to jump, I stood on the edge of the boat, terribly miscast, unable to take the next step. I never jumped. But rereading today's notification, I had to reconsider. Perhaps ExWhy was right and I shouldn't give up.

I wrestled with this when there was the expected knock at the door. "It's open!" I shouted.

Ellen took two steps into the apartment, leaned against the wall and slid down to sit on the floor. Jerry, right behind her, closed the door and stepped over her without looking. Ellen took out her ExWhy Pod and became absorbed by ExWhy-centric activity.

"What's up with her?" I asked Jerry, who joined me in the living room.

He paused by the open window to gaze at the cityscape, then plopped like a sack of potatoes onto his usual spot on the couch, slung his feet up on the coffee table, and exhaled. "We just came back from that new restaurant I suggested. It's around the corner on Rosemont."

I thought for a moment. "Oh, that one with the letters... T.G.I. – ",

He inserted: "—T.G.I.Faraday's."

"*Faraday's?* That's an odd name... Sounds like another chain."

"But it's not. Big-time, this one is not".

Ellen muttered to herself, "No-no-no. Shit!" which prompted Jerry to chuckle. He continued, "This one's in a basement. Nice ambiance with the usual novelties hanging on the walls and ceiling. Typical American cuisine. But... and this is the kicker... it's a Faraday Cage."

I nodded along until he got to the last words. "Faraday Cage?"

He glanced back at muttering Ellen with a smirk that turned into a grin. "They really ought to have a disclaimer out front. Maybe customers should sign a waiver first. Some people were freaking out."

"*Faraday Cage?*" I repeated, with emphasis.

"Oh, sorry, yeah. Within the walls and ceiling is a metallic mesh that blocks transmission of radio waves. So, no Internet access. Their tag line is 'Take a vacation from information.' The upstairs lobby was crowded, standing room only, not with people waiting to be seated, but with diners interrupting their meals to come upstairs for information hits... like chain smokers stepping out for their puffs."

As I processed this, Ellen cheered, "Yes! All caught up." She stood, restored, and strode into the living room. A broad smile flashed when she saw me: "Hi, Chuck!", with a little wave.

I nodded. "Hi... Hey, how was dinner?"

She hardened. "Never again." Turning to Jerry, she blurted, "Are you out of your mind?" Jerry burst into laughter, prompting her evil glare.

I played dumb. "But I heard the food was good... No?"

Ellen replied in a small voice, "Mine got cold".

That triggered Jerry. "You couldn't sit still! Up the stairs, then down for a bite, and then up. Jeez, you couldn't even order without input from your ExWhy Pod."

She shot back, "I wanted to enjoy my meal!"

"So did I!" he countered. "Maybe with some company!"

Ellen pivoted to direct her appeal to me. Her anger was barely contained, like rapidly boiling water in a pot covered by a heavy lid. Fierce sideways glances at Jerry were like angry blasts of venting steam. "ExWhy knows what I like and what each restaurant serves. It knows what I've eaten and keeps track of my calories and nutrition. It knows my weight goals." She gripped the ExWhy Pod so tight that her knuckles were white peaks about to pop through taut skin, if she didn't crush the device first. She took a breath. "But that place keeps everyone in the dark!"

I nodded, innocent and sympathetic. "Oh my, so I've heard." Jerry twisted toward me, looking more annoyed than perplexed.

Ellen cooled, as if confidence washed away the fury. "One more thing," now directing a laser-like focus at Jerry with piercing eyes, "ExWhy knows *who* I like."

"And what the *hell* does *that* mean?" barked Jerry.

"It couldn't track our dinner tonight, but I just updated it—about everything. Newsflash: ExWhy knows that we are finished!" she announced, with a dramatic sweep of her ExWhy hand.

Jerry pointed at the ExWhy Pod, seething. "You're going to stand there and tell me that thing is breaking us up?"

"It knows me better than you do! *So much better!* It would never recommend T.G.I.Faraday's!"

"Of course it wouldn't! When you're down there, it can't have your brain in its..." He struggled for words, "... plastic grip!" He frowned momentarily, apparently disappointed with the metaphor, but then stood and announced, "Fine!" He marched toward the door as he shouted, "I hope the two of you will be very happy!" Then he swung the door open and flew out with a slam.

We stared at the closed door as dust settled. Although I had maintained outward composure, this drama sent my heart racing. I could see Ellen's chest heaving as she caught her breath, but she didn't appear to be sobbing. As we calmed, she turned to me. The ExWhy death grip was relaxed and she seemed uplifted.

She glided toward the couch and, without breaking her gaze, settled on Jerry's place. Her face glowed. "How could Jerry have known?"

I tilted my head, which made her giggle, puzzling me further.

"He hoped the two of us would be very happy. How could Jerry have known that ExWhy told me I should be with you?"

My ExWhy Pod vibrated. I slipped my hand into my pocket to discretely peek. A relationship alert blinked: "Date Ellen!" against a gaudy backdrop of animated hearts and cupids. I jerked out my hand as if there was a scorpion in my pocket.

Ellen beamed with anticipation.

I slowly folded my hands in my lap, attempting to exude nonchalance. I hadn't felt much attraction to Ellen. She and Jerry had been a couple for years. This was reason enough to keep my distance. And, even for my tastes, Ellen was an ExWhy addict. Jerry, on the other hand, not only shunned the device, but I had even seen him use a paper map. As far as ExWhy was concerned, he was off-grid except for Ellen's updates.

"You're acting coy," she gushed. "That's *cute!*" She clutched my hands and scooted next to me.

I wanted to be free of this woman but ExWhy egged me on. Sure, Jerry was out of the picture now, and ExWhy, truth be told, knew me pretty well. But then I flashed back to that scene on the side of boat, looking between my flippers at slate gray, wind-rippled waves. I recalled ExWhy Pod's message: "Take the plunge!" I had felt like the intrepid first penguin to leap off a glacier, pecked into action by the colony that feared a lurking killer whale.

Ellen gazed at me, dreamy, with those sky blue eyes.

My ExWhy Pod vibrated again. "Sorry... ExWhy." I pulled my hand away to look. Ellen excused any ExWhy interruption. I peered into my pocket and was shocked to see, "Take the plunge!"

"Chucky!" she teased. I hated that name. She gave my hand an extra squeeze.

From somewhere unfathomably deep I was able to access common sense, precious and rare. I responded with feigned disappointment. "Sorry, Ellen, but my ExWhy has someone else in mind."

Ellen was crestfallen but then perplexed, probably by the apparent ExWhy inconsistency. I added, with the liveliness of a freed prisoner, "But it says we should still stay friends!"

She brightened, "So, who knows!?"

"Right…" My ExWhy Pod vibrated with its incessant command as Ellen stared with urgent expectation.

I needed a way out.

I withdrew the device from my pocket and then switched it off. Ellen's face fell; she pulled away and sat back, deflated. Her lip curled into a little pout and she fixed her gaze on an empty place on the table. It was chilling, as though I had turned off the muse that animated her affections for me.

I walked to the open window. She watched and I felt her eyes on me, like invisible fingers, clinging.

Then I flung the device out. She cried, "No! Why?"

I turned to her and declared, "It had to take the plunge."

THE HEART
OF THE ICE

As the sun slipped below the crater rim, a bank of lights illuminated the roadside sign: "Welcome to Haworth Crater Ops / Polar Oasis Ltd Mechanical Exclusivity Zone." A compact shuttle rolled past the sign and into the compound. Dust flared up in its wake and promptly returned to the lunar surface. In the shuttle, Elisabeth turned away from her eReader to glance out the window. She returned to the book in a race to finish the chapter before the shuttle arrived.

The shuttle slowed and maneuvered to the center of the compound. The chapter complete, Elisabeth secured her helmet as perfunctory announcements were made and the vehicle stopped. The cabin depressurized and the few passengers disembarked. Elisabeth knew the short walk well. She thought she could make it blindfolded, if perhaps the lights went out and the compound was cast into unfathomable blackness. That kind of darkness was rare in the solar system, found in places never reached by sunlight such as this outpost at the Moon's south pole. She reached the entrance of the Operations Dispatch Building, which looked more like a tin foil igloo than a proper building.

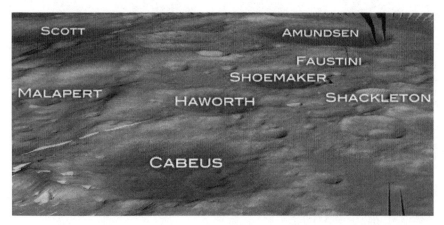

Lunar South Pole by Lunar Reconnaissance Orbiter (credit: NASA)

The airlock had the basic Vacant/Occupied indicator above the latch. This always reminded her of a toilet on a spaceplane, except an airlock had less than half the volume and no seat. Such minimalist airlocks were ubiquitous; strictly standing room only. A quick twist of her wrist and the latch slid from Vacant to Occupied. The door opened with an inaudible swoosh as the small pocket of trapped air escaped. She stepped in and the tiny chamber began to pressurize. This took several minutes and she used the time to scan the dispatch floor to size up the other miners gathered for today's assignments. There were five miners, three men and two women, all seated in helmet-free comfort, killing time while they waited, engaged in animated conversations that were silent to her in the partial vacuum of the airlock. Who would she be paired with? Most were regulars, somewhat tolerable, but there was a new face and that could be trouble.

Above the dispatcher's window glowed a red sign that set the cadence for the room and all of Polar Oasis Ltd.: The current spot price of new lunar water. As she watched, it ticked up $5 to $1,985/kg; higher than average, but she'd seen it push $3000/kg. Demand for new water was dominated by the need for hydrogen and oxygen fuel for propellant, essential for lunar mining and industry. Water for drinking, washing, and even some for agriculture was renewable and was recycled. But the lunar economy was export-based; hydrogen-and-oxygen propellant was a critical yet non-renewable resource needed to deliver the goods. Still far too expensive to supply from

Earth, water was trapped in the eternally shaded craters of the south pole, but locked in ancient regolith in often trace amounts. It had to be mined, actually scraped, and then smelted. Hence, a dispatch room of miners of generally class Scraper I or II.

The airlock pressure was now sufficient to conduct sound and Elisabeth could barely begin to hear talking and occasional laughter. It was a gentle way to reconnect to social life among a group. So much time was spent in near solitude, alone or with only one other miner piloting a scraper or on a haul to Malapert to deliver a load for assay and smelting. Elisabeth was a private person who didn't suffer fools gladly. Alas, it seemed to her as if the south pole attracted more than its share of fools in search of quick riches, and they often learned the ropes as miners employed by Polar. Because Elisabeth was among the most experienced Scrapers, she'd be saddled with them on mining runs, ostensibly as a "mentor," but rare was the partner worth the effort. Yet even she occasionally longed for more time with others.

With pressurization, the sound grew louder; there were bursts of laughter, but they were all in the same voice. She smiled at first but then noticed that the laughing person was a man who sat alone; the face she didn't recognize.

The airlock fully pressurized, and the latch automatically opened into the dispatch room. This always stopped conversation and made for a dramatic entrance. Five heads turned with expectant smiles, but when they saw who it was, four quickly turned back to their conversations. Elisabeth wasn't surprised by the four; she'd worked with them before and the sentiments were assuredly mutual. Only the loud laugher continued to look, grinning. He was a stout man, in his mid-30s, like she, and maybe six feet tall or about six inches taller than she. His sky-blue pressure suit revealed a modest paunch. She didn't even know suits came in that color; hers was standard-issue silver. Elisabeth lifted her helmet visor and managed a brief smile in his direction. The smell of bad office coffee partially masked the odor of burnt gunpowder, the only scent that the Moon had to offer from the tracked-in dust.

The dispatcher appeared at the window and cleared his throat, which drew everyone's undivided attention. "OK, I have requisitions for three teams. And we now have six Scrapers." He glanced down at a display. She'd gotten assignments here many times and it drove her crazy how this dispatcher often said "OK" for no reason.

"OK, first, Elisabeth Snyder and Gray Walker?" He looked up to see Elisabeth and, as she feared, the laugher, approach the window.

"OK, so you two are assigned to Cabeus Crater, quadrant 3. It's a new field, no mining there yet, so you'll have a lot of boulders to clear out. Looks like there might by 0.6% water in some places. Then take your load to Malapert for assay and smelting, OK? Gray, here, is a Scraper II recently promoted from Scraper I. Elisabeth, here, has been a Scraper II for years. So, you'll make a great team." He slid a small sheet of holographic plastic which Elisabeth grabbed. "That's your proof of claim to present at Malapert. Get going. Next..." then he went on to the next pair of miners.

"Hi, Elisabeth, I'm Gray Walker! Glad to meet you!" Her newly-assigned partner beamed.

Elisabeth learned long ago to put up a strong defense when meeting someone new. She deflected his wave of emotion with, "Hi."

He dipped his head to speak into a mouthpiece above his collarbone, while still maintaining eye contact with her. "Hey, Paul, call you back." He chuckled.

A second radio in his suit for personal communication, she thought. Interesting. At least he isn't psycho.

Gray went back to the bench to pick up his helmet. He looked forward to getting to know his new colleague. The social scene at the south pole was often compared to a co-ed submarine. Nobody was raising a family here and Polar Oasis, the only local employer, frowned upon marriage between employees. So, while there was a lively dating scene, the nature of the work demanded professionalism. Gray thrived on this social chemistry. His free time was often spent with friends he'd met on the job; in fact, he sought the promotion from Scraper I because he had grown too old for his 20-something colleagues. It had become clear to him (and to them) that they were on a different timeline, and that was fine. To be teamed with an attractive woman on his first assignment as Scraper II seemed like kismet, but one advantage of being in his mid-30s was that he knew not to get spun up by a pretty face.

He placed the sky-blue helmet over his head and secured it to his suit, visor up. Turning back to Elisabeth, he continued, "I spent a year scraping over at Amundsen. You know, it's pretty smooth terrain over there. Great for a Scraper I, but it's rather picked over. We were only seeing 0.1%. Hardly worth charging the batteries on the scraper. I was looking for something new so I applied for Scraper II and here I am! What's your story?"

She wasn't going to tell him her "story," so she replied with, "I'll pilot the scraper. Get a truck with five trailers… no, make that six. I'll meet you at the compound gate." Gray looked like he wanted to say something, so she added, "Let's get out of here before there's a line." She tilted her head toward the airlock.

"OK! We had a 4-person airlock at Amundsen."

"Uh huh. And we'll talk on Channel B. If your friends use that channel, tell them to change."

"We use Channel C." He smiled throughout the brusque exchange; the expression reminded her of the permanent smile on a cat or a dolphin. Something that had to smile.

The scraper was like the mega-machine combines that swept across the Great Plains at harvest time. It was a caterpillar track vehicle. Mounted to the front was a 10-meter wide scraper head, which was in a stowed configuration for transit to Cabeus, 40 kilometers away. Within the scraper head were four titanium blades that, when deployed, scraped away the top layer of the regolith and channeled the material into a holding bay. When full, the bay was dumped into one of the trailers towed by the truck.

The truck looked more like a bulldozer, with a blade in front not for scraping but to push boulders and clear the field for the scraper. The vehicle was mounted high above three axles that swiveled to roll over irregular, rock strewn terrain.

Elisabeth, in the scraper, rolled to the gate first and waited. Gray soon followed in the truck with trailers. Even though his vehicle hadn't even slowed, she asserted authority: "Let's go."

"OK!" came the bright reply.

The caravan rolled away from the compound on the highland service road that wound its way between and along crater rims to Cabeus. The road was unimproved, in fact rarely used, and only recently had Polar Oasis Ltd. installed wireless repeaters. Ahead of the scraper, in pitch darkness or high contrast shadows, the rugged surface was scanned in different frequencies. This painted the landscape to aid navigation, the focus of Elisabeth's attention.

Gray, however, only had a view of the rear of the scraper. "This will be a bit of a ride, a few hours, I guess. What shall we talk about?" No reply. "And do you go by Betty? Beth? Betsy?"

"Elisabeth. Let's just concentrate on getting to Cabeus in one piece."

Gray bit his lip to keep from giving his partner a piece of his mind. "It's a living," he muttered to himself, but it was transmitted to Elisabeth, who ignored it.

Elisabeth guided the scraper through a pass in the rim of Cabeus Crater. While the crater's base was more rugged than most, Cabeus was ancient and its walls were considerably worn. This made for straightforward ingress to quadrant 3. The convoy reached the base of the crater and settled on a level staging area.

Elisabeth jumped out and began prospecting with a handheld X-ray element analyzer. "Start clearing!"

He didn't reply; his timeless smile briefly disappeared. *She had to tell me that?*

The quadrant was studded with large boulders. Gray unhitched the truck and, smiling again, hollered "Tally ho!" as he aimed the truck at his first rock. Elisabeth ignored the distraction and focused on prospecting.

Several boulders later, Gray attempted professional banter to normalize the partnership. "What kind of concentrations are you picking up?"

"It varies."

"OK, between what and what?" This was like pulling teeth.

Elisabeth didn't answer, preferring to interact with the instrument in her hand rather than with her partner. Gray began to fume, his smile negated. Finally, she offered, "I got a 1.3%."

"Wow, that's fantastic!"

"It was just one spot."

He gave up and concentrated on the remaining boulders. After 30 minutes of this tedium, he spoke up, but it was to reconnect with his friend on Channel C. Alas, his mute switch for Channel B had a loose connection. Elisabeth heard a staticky click, then, "Hey Paul... You there?" She tried to ignore the conversation. "Cool... listen, I am working with an ice queen here." Laughter. "No, not queen of finding ice." Laughter. "Worse than her... way worse!" Elisabeth grimaced and tried to pay attention to the prospecting. Gray continued, "I was thinking about the project. I agree that it's risky, but I think... I think it's worth the risk. We can pull this off." A long pause, then, "Exactly. Get started, but keep it under wraps. Then, bam! Everyone will know." Laughter. "Yeah, we need mechanical exclusivity! OK, I gotta get back to the ice queen. Later." Laughter, then a staticky click. "Hey, E-lis-a-beth, just one more and I'll be done here."

The intercepted conversation stopped Elisabeth in her tracks. All she could manage was, "OK." In the pitch-black basin of the crater, she stared at the lights on the busy truck. *'Bam?' 'Everyone will know?' What the hell is this project?* But then she caught herself. Like a rogue wave, a new insight crashed ashore. She reflected on her entrance to the Dispatch Building, on the routine of rejection and loneliness. It seemed like every encounter with a new person had an inflection point that triggered a death spiral. It happened with each of the four miners in the Dispatch Building. And this was the inflection point with Gray, but maybe, just maybe, she could postpone the inevitable.

Gray plowed loose the boulder, causing it to roll down a gentle slope. "Yes!"

Elisabeth looked up. "Yo! That just rolled into quadrant 2."

He bristled at the "Yo!" The boulder error seemed excusable even for an experienced Scraper II, so this time he decided return the volley: "Yo! I thought I pushed it hard enough to roll through to the wall on the other side of 2. Yo! I'll push it out. Yo! OK?"

It was rare for a newbie to talk back, but this was comical and, mindful of the inflection point, Elisabeth chose to play along. "Leave it... yo!" She crunched the relationship calculus and, emboldened, pushed the envelope: "I'm going to start rolling the scraper. Ever ridden on one of these new M Class rigs? You're welcome to ride along during the test run."

Gray counted this as true progress, fully aware that, as a terminal optimist, he had to proceed with caution. "Sure!"

Elisabeth and Gray climbed the ladder several meters up into the cabin and were soon seated in its relative pressurized comfort. They removed their helmets and Elisabeth turned her attention to the pilot console. With a tap, an array of floodlights illuminated the area ahead and then she deployed the huge scraper header. Gray picked up the claim ticket that was tucked in a dashboard pocket, but that triggered a reflex from Elisabeth: "Put that back." Perhaps it was uncalled for but she wasn't ready to release the reins just yet.

"I'm just looking at it." He tilted the plastic and watched the hologram of the Moon rotate, a corporate tagline floating overhead. The giant scraper motors began to vibrate the entire structure. Gray read the tagline out loud: "Polar Oasis Ltd. Mechanical Exclusivity Zone." Elisabeth ignored him, as he continued, "Robber barons. The Moon is nobody's property."

She replied, eyes still looking ahead. "Nobody claimed it as *property*. Polar Oasis started mining and they aren't about to share. It's first-come first-served, which is easier to understand than 'mechanical exclusivity.' Same thing." She flipped a switch and a new, shrill whine emerged from deep below them. "I just extended the blades. And, besides..." she turned to him, "it's a living." That last phrase landed; maybe work was the same grind for her as it was for him. Gray put back the ticket and turned his attention to Elisabeth's piloting. She put the scraper in gear. With a sudden shove, the behemoth began to lumber forward.

As they slowly bumped along, the console displayed the status of ore deposited into the holding bay behind the cabin. "Good stuff," said Elisabeth. The path ahead was fairly level, so she throttled the motors and the scraper picked up speed. The holding bay was filling with high grade ore.

Status indicators were all green, when there was a sudden deafening crack. The scraper lurched to the left as Elisabeth and Gray pitched to the right, held in place by their seat belts. A wide spray of dust swept ahead of the vehicle. The console glowed red. Elisabeth cut the power to the motors and the scraper was suddenly silent and still.

She turned to Gray, with a grave expression: "We hit a boulder."

Gray gesticulated, "Look out there; perfectly flat!"

"Well, you missed it and I bet we have busted blades." She put on her helmet. "Suit up; we need to check out the damage."

Elisabeth was first down to the surface. Switching on her spotlight, she turned to the undercarriage. "Find out what we hit. I'll assess the damage."

Gray took the direction. From behind the scraper, he walked along a deep gouge and followed it to a shallow pit. Across the bottom, his light illuminated a partial slice through freshly exposed rock a couple of meters in diameter. At the end of the shiny slice was a meter-long hunk of once-precisely machined titanium scraper blade now twisted and bent upright, standing like a postmodern sundial in a place where no sunlight would ever fall. In the background, Elisabeth muttered, "This is totaled."

Gray knelt and examined the rock. "That was no boulder. That was the tip of a subsurface breccia formation."

She shined her light toward Gray and saw him next to the improbable metal shape poking out of the ground. She looked back at the gnarled blade remains under the scraper. Primal leadership elbowed its way to the fore. "Do you think it matters whether or not it was boulder?" adding, to herself, "Idiot," which, of course, Gray heard.

His blood reached the boiling point. "Listen! I don't know what *idiots* you may have worked with before, but that was then and this is now... and this *me*. Do you have X-Ray vision? Would you have seen that subsurface structure?" Fed up, he marched back to the scraper to confront her.

His words struck like a thunderbolt. In any other circumstance, such as with the four miners, she'd dish it out and they'd take it, a toxic role play of the know-it-all mentor and submissive trainees. Now it was going to happen yet again, except Gray wasn't going to play along. Elisabeth decided to break the cycle. As he arrived, she raised her palms as though to stop him. "You're right. In fact, that happened to me once at Shackleton." He stood and felt his blood start to cool. Then, she added a little, "Yo," punctuated with a smile. He flashed a grin. It was uplifting to come clean, to assert control over the inflection point. Empowered, she added, "I'm sorry."

He exhaled the head of steam. "I was starting to wonder if you were human inside that suit. It's OK."

She extended her hand to shake, in a comically exaggerated gesture of good will; he played along. Then she added, "Get the truck and hitch one trailer. I'm going to remove the rest of the broken blades and we'll take it all to Malapert for replacements."

─────

By the time Gray drove the truck and trailer to the scraper, there was a waiting pile of titanium scrap. The mangled blades gleamed in the headlights, behind which Elisabeth stood. As he climbed out of the cabin, Gray noticed that the sundial was still in place. "Do we want to recycle the part sticking up over there?"

"Let's leave it as a hazard marker; plus, Polar may want to investigate the accident. I would have been demoted after Shackleton without evidence."

Few words were spoken as they worked together to lift the long, twisted blades and other scrap into the trailer. Then, Gray walked around the truck to the driver side, but before he could climb in, Elisabeth declared, "I'll drive."

"This is ridiculous. I can drive."

"It's not personal, it's protocol. The lead drives crater ingress and egress and, with just one vehicle, I drive."

"Ok," Gray assented.

The truck and trailer pulled away from the disabled scraper and up the gentle slope of Cabeus crater, bound for Malapert. The pressurized cabin was comfortable and, with their budding familiarity, Elisabeth and Gray engaged in small talk, a staple of Gray's social diet. For Elisabeth, however, small talk had always been garnish to brush aside. But here, with Gray, it nourished her anemic spirit.

The initial climb was smooth and monotonous. After a while, small talk ended and as the kilometers rolled by, Gray nodded off. Elisabeth slowed to study him, peaceful, with the always-smile and in that silly blue pressure suit. She wanted to bookmark the little happy scene. With a tender look, she continued the drive.

The monotony made the trek taxing. Even though scanners helped to point the way, steady concentration was needed on the uncharted journey. Gray's repose was contagious and Elisabeth's eyelids began to droop. Suddenly, an alarm blared, "Warning: Hazard ahead!" They were shocked into full attention to see that the terrain had changed and the truck was headed for a drop-off. Elisabeth whipped the steering wheel around, which caused the trailer to rock then pitch onto its side. As the trailer dragged, she slammed the brakes and the truck stopped just short of the brink.

They stared at each other, jolted. "I fell asleep," confessed Elisabeth.

"Well, I beat you to it. I think everything is OK, but we should…"

She had turned to look at the trailer through the rear window. "Uh oh. Trailer flipped. Put on your helmet."

The contents of the trailer were strewn down the cliffside, lost forever. In the low gravity, they were able to right the trailer, which seemed intact. Gray started to walk toward the driver's side. "I think it's time for changing the guard."

"It's yours."

━━━━━━

They still had a long journey ahead to Malapert, much of it outside the Mechanical Exclusivity Zone, so road conditions would remain uncertain—assuming there even were roads on this side of Cabeus. At the crest of Cabeus, Gray stopped the truck to assess their location. In the distance ahead and to the right was Malapert Mountain, their destination, visible forever because its altitude lifted it into permanent sunlight. The fact that it was practically paved with solar panels gave it a brilliant shimmer. Its eternal illumination made Malapert the ideal center for energy intensive operations such as smelting and separating water into hydrogen and oxygen. On nearby plateaus, fields of gargantuan freestanding panels rotated with the Moon to maintain constant solar exposure.

With no road, Gray drove slowly down the outer rim slope. The sun was due left and the truck and trailer cast long black shadows to the right. As they rolled downhill, the sun slipped behind a ridge, revealing the stunning corona that fanned high above the horizon. The headlights turned on as the truck descended into pitch-black shadow; Malapert shimmered above the shaded landscape far to the right. He noticed a sign posted on a nearby sunlit promontory. The sign faced Cabeus, but it could still be read from here with a scope. He slowed to a stop and began to reach for the scope, but instead asked Elisabeth. "Hey, can you check that out?"

With a cheery, "Sure!" she stared at the sign through the scope. "Leaving Polar Oasis Ltd. Mechanical Exclusivity Zone / Entering Lunar Open Zone." Gray looked puzzled. She continued, "It means we are in no man's land. No robber barons have claimed anything out here yet. Oh, that also means no repeaters, so you can't talk to your friend."

She pointed to Malapert and commanded, "Go *that* way," but a new reflex snapped and she added, "I mean, since there are no roads out here, we may as well aim for the mountain, OK?"

"Yeah, I was just looking for a good path."

"And we'll dip in and out of shade so be careful." Then she offered, "Let me know if you want me to drive," which prompted Gray to turn to her and chuckle. "What's so funny?!" Gray burst into laughter and she playfully punched him on the shoulder. "Stop it! One little mistake and now you won't let me live it down!"

The playful punches continued amid laughter and she made a grin from gritting teeth. She tried to look fierce, but Gray saw an adorable face. He put his arms around her, as though to stop the punches. "OK, stop. You win. I promise that I won't say that you almost drove us over a cliff." She returned the hug, gazed into his eyes, and kissed him. She slid as close to him as her seatbelt would permit and wrapped her arm around his.

Gray felt electrified, but still somewhat in the dark about Elisabeth even as he roamed the polar darkness. Both situations called for careful navigation. He gingerly turned the truck on the incline and proceeded with Malapert straight ahead. Headlights pierced the blackness and the scanners painted the scene in their many frequencies. The terrain was strewn with boulders that Gray ably negotiated in the inky darkness.

After cautiously maneuvering through the boulder field, Gray was relieved that the scanners now showed the way ahead to be fairly smooth and rising out of the shade to a sunlit crest. He pressed the accelerator and the vehicle sped across the regolith. They were on their way to make great time. Elisabeth's arm still around his, they shared the magic of this journey through uncharted territory.

The truck began the steepening climb toward the sunlit crest, which felt like a rocket launch as they were pressed into their seats. All signs were clear and Elisabeth giggled. It was thrilling. They crossed into the sunlight and a moment later to the top of the crest, when they were blinded by the almost nuclear brilliance of glare from every solar panel at Malapert that faced the sun, now directly behind them. They both screamed and covered their eyes.

The rocketing truck and trailer sailed over the top of the crest, which was merely a sharp peak, and soared as the other side of the peak receded below them into the shade. To the shock of blindness was now added weightlessness. Elisabeth and Gray groped for helmets that had begun to float. There had been no safety drill for this scenario; they secured helmets and braced for the unseen impact.

The concussion came as a one-two kick rather than a single crash, with the vehicle was now mercifully at rest, albeit tipped forward a bit.

They caught their breath and, vision restored, looked at each other... then burst into laughter, not only from profound relief of having survived, but because they were wearing each other's helmet. Elisabeth, with "Gray" written above her visor, said, "It suits you." He was amused at the sight of her wearing a sky-blue helmet and replied, "You never looked better." While the cabin was still pressurized, they kept their helmets on; nothing was visible through the dust-covered windows, making assessment of their situation almost impossible.

For Elisabeth, levity was soon replaced by mounting urgency; the opaque windows made the cabin walls feel as if they were closing in. "I don't like this, Gray." Her mind leapt to stories of early lunar explorers who didn't know if they'd be swallowed by dust. It terrified her. Who knew what hazards lie undiscovered? Frantic, she pounded on her door's window to dislodge the dust coating outside. A little avalanche cleared a gap through which a rock face was visible, but only centimeters away. She made a whimpering noise and turned to Gray. "We're buried alive!"

"We don't know that. Chill." He reached to hold her hands. Her fast breathing slowed and her eyes softened as they looked into his. He continued. "One thing at a time. Let's depressurize… um, starting with the *cabin*."

She got the joke, a tiny wash of relief, and squeezed his hands.

The cabin depressurized but they found that neither door could swing open far enough to climb out. Elisabeth kept trying, crashing her door into the rock, which alarmed Gray. "Stop! You'll damage the seal." When Gray opened his door, after some debris fell, he leaned his head into the gap to peer skyward. "OK, I see stars, so we aren't buried alive. That's progress." He gestured behind the seat. "This truck has a roof hatch." He clambered over the seat to a small storage space and then released latches in the ceiling. He pushed open the hatch, squeezed himself out, and Elisabeth scrambled behind him, thrilled to escape the cabin. They stood on the truck's roof, which was littered with dust and small rocks, but neither expected the scene in front of the truck.

The headlights illuminated a rough tunnel, about three meters in diameter, that stretched ahead maybe 25 meters before curving away. "Lava tube," said Gray, shaking his head in disbelief. "We broke through the surface and into a lava tube. Incredible. That probably saved our lives."

Looking behind, they saw that the trailer remained hitched and rested on a partially collapsed section of the lava tube. That presented a precarious path back to the surface. "We can try to back up the ramp," said Gray.

With liberation from the cabin, Elisabeth relaxed. She studied Gray as he surveyed the scene. "Sorry I freaked out in there. There's just something about buried alive that I never liked. Can't put my finger on it."

He shined a flashlight down the tunnel. "No accounting for taste. Don't worry about it."

"And… I guess we're even now," making a pantomime of the crashing truck. She walked over and put her arms around him, enjoying the freedom of not being constrained by seatbelts.

He returned the hug. "You know, you're way too hard on yourself, Elisabeth."

"I may even be too hard on others."

Gray looked down at her with a mock expression of shock. "Do ya think?"

She made the adorable fierce expression to give another punch, but decided instead to gesture at the walls of the pit to say, "I'm glad we're in this together!" Here, in a collapsed lava tube with Gray, she paradoxically felt safer than she had in years. "OK, let's get on our way to Malapert!"

But Gray had other ideas. He stepped from the roof down to the hood to hop off the truck. Elisabeth watched, alarmed as he walked away from the truck and into the tunnel. "Where are you going?"

"I want to explore. The lava tube is a beauty!" The passage was easily tall enough for him to walk upright.

But Elisabeth imagined the worst, a catastrophe that would teach her once and for all never to let her guard down. "Don't leave me," she said in a small voice.

He looked up at the compact woman standing in silhouette before the glorious Milky Way that swept vertically across the black sky. Elisabeth was bright and demanding, complex and warm. Those parts came together like puzzle pieces… with him. "Don't worry; I won't be far. I'll be back soon."

"OK, but wait a sec." She bounded down next to him to give a tight hug which he returned. She enjoyed being this close to him and looked up. "I have a little confession. That smile of yours used to piss me off."

He leaned back, perplexed. "Why?"

"It was like you smiled for no reason." Her arms still around him, she gazed up at the splash of stars. It felt so free to be unwound, unbound. "Now, I think it was I who had no reason... for not smiling." They hugged again.

Elisabeth watched him walk away into the darkness, until he disappeared around the curve. "Be careful."

Gray scanned the dull, charcoal hued passage with his light as he advanced. The floor was under a layer of fine dust, from which he presumed the tube was ancient. That meant it was stable, at least when not smashed by a truck and trailer. He saw that the wall composition was fairly uniform, as expected, when up ahead a shiny, almost glassy, streak caught the light and glinted in the blackness. As he approached, he followed the vein with his flashlight. Far up the wall, it began as a slender irregular translucent line that widened considerably as it traversed the wall before it disappeared, meters wide, under the floor dust. He stepped next to the vein to explore the material with his flashlight, shining into it from different angles to observe how it scattered and refracted the bright beam. The beam penetrated deep into the nearly transparent material. His heart pounded. "Come here! And bring your gun!"

"What? Are you OK? What gun?"

"That thing you use for prospecting. And bring a crowbar! And a big hammer! You'll find tools in the cabinet behind the cabin; it should be easy to reach."

"Why?"

"Please just *do* it!" While he waited for Elisabeth, Gray brushed away the floor dust to expose a broad nearly flat translucent patch. His light beam shone down into the material, which was so crystal clear that features of the containing rock were visible meters beneath him. It's probably just quartz, he told himself. He had to stop fantasizing, stop from leaping to the possibilities of what it meant if this was... *ice*.

A second light beam flashed and he turned to see Elisabeth. The X-ray element analyzer was strapped to her belt; she carried a sledgehammer, with the crowbar tucked under her arm. He saw her reaction to the incredulous site. There was Gray, kneeling, shining his light into a luminous patch of the floor. He looked up at her and smiled from beneath the "Elisabeth" written above his visor.

"Gray, what have you found!?" She unclipped the analyzer and dropped the sledgehammer and crowbar. He didn't reply, waiting for the analyzer to answer the question. She knelt next to him and pointed the gun at the patch. They watched as the display quickly responded: $H_2O... 100\%$. Her hand shook. Gray followed as she pointed at another spot on the floor. Same result. Up the wall, she pointed at spot after spot, each returning the same remarkable result until she couldn't contain her excitement and burst into uncontrollable laughter. This snapped Gray's anticipation and triggered him to shout, "We're rich! We are filthy rich!"

"Gray, is your Channel C off? Turn it off."

"It's off, but nobody can pick up a signal from here... inside a lava tube... in no man's land."

She realized this was true, but added, "You know what this means? We can claim this. We can mine this, take it to Malapert. But nobody can find out about this before we file a claim."

"Do you really think Polar would allow us to claim this? Those robber barons would be tearing this place up the day after tomorrow." As she considered this, Gray demonstrated his sledgehammer prowess as if swinging a baseball bat. "Ice is like rock at this temperature." He reached toward the sledgehammer. "Gimme. You hold the crowbar against the ice and I'll try to crack it."

Her imagination raced, first with the thrill of the discovery, but also with trepidation at holding a crowbar while it was whacked by a sledgehammer. *When in doubt, act rationally.* She passed Gray the sledgehammer, stooped down to the ice with the crowbar, and paused to follow the heavy steel head through the practice swings. "You know, Gray, if it was anyone else, there's no way I would do this. I don't care how much ice there was."

He knelt down, put hand on her shoulder, and gave a gentle squeeze. "There is no way I could hurt you."

She clutched his hand. "OK, let's do this." They took their positions. Her trembling hand shook the crowbar as she held it against the ice.

Gray prepared to swing but balked. "Hey, you have to keep it still." She gripped the crowbar with both of her trembling hands and, together, they kept the crowbar reasonably still.

He stood and took a couple slow practice swings to ensure a clean strike. With clenched eyes, she waited. In a spasm it was over. She felt fragments hitting her suit. She opened her eyes. Chunks of ice!

"Super!" shouted Gray. "Well done!"

Elisabeth exhaled. The strike sent deep fractures into the ice and excavated a small crater. "Wow."

Gray picked up a piece and studied it in the palm of his hand. "This is about a quarter kilogram. What's the spot price? About $2000? So, that makes this worth..."

"Five... hundred... dollars" she said, transfixed by the lump.

Now it was Gray's turn to say, "Wow."

"Listen," said Gray, "Polar's going to wonder what happened to us. We have to move fast before they come looking, if they haven't already."

Elisabeth's executive brain asserted control. There was a job to do. "Let's get cracking!" She positioned the crowbar in the small crater, aligned with a fracture.

Gray picked up the sledgehammer. "Why not pick a fresh spot?"

"We want to treat this like a diamond. Strike at the fractures, the flaws, and that should shatter more of it into pieces that can be removed."

Gray swung and a connected squarely with the crowbar, sending fracture lines deep into the ice and liberating chunks near the surface. Elisabeth repositioned the crowbar. "Perfect. Do that again." Whack! Another clear strike filled the growing crater with loose ice. From her kneeling position, Elisabeth scooped the ice out of the pit,. "Fifty-fifty split... agreed?"

"Of course, sweetheart!"

Elisabeth's soul was catapulted. *Sweetheart*. She beamed.

The duo continued in a rhythm that soon yielded a significant pile of pure ice, yet it was still only a start of the floor excavation. Gray stopped to catch his breath. "You know, I wonder why this wasn't found during the reconnaissance surveys that turned up the other ice fields."

"I was thinking about that, too," said Elisabeth, sitting next to the pile. "It helped that this was in a lava tube, but it is also such a small footprint. They searched for oceans and missed a spring."

Gray nodded in agreement. "How much do we mine? If they show up, we'll have nothing. You know that, right?" She nodded. "And another thing, a find this large may drop the spot price... a lot. Who knows how deep this spring goes." Pointing to the pile, he added, "That may be the last $2000 lunar ice."

"Another hour and we stop." said Elisabeth. "We have to haul this to the trailer and back it out... we don't have much time." She repositioned the crowbar and Gray, refreshed, swung a mighty blow that sent several giant chunks loose. They continued at a frenzied pace, carving wider and deeper into the floor. They even tried the narrower wall vein, which dislodged huge slabs, but the exposed fissure made the deeper ice unreachable. So, without any spoken communication, they returned to the floor, methodically circumscribing the hole, striking along fault lines that widened the pit. Elisabeth scooped out ice while Gray caught his breath. With the frenetic pace and the time pressure, there was no giggling, no happy talk. This was the chance of a lifetime and that meant there was only one thing to do... and they did it together.

At last, Gray sat, exhausted. "That's all I got. It's an hour, by definition." The mountain of accumulated ice was several cubic meters, several thousand kilograms.

Elisabeth checked the time. "Close enough. Stay and rest, my dear; I'll get the tarp to load this so we can drag it to the truck." *My dear*. She said the words but heard them as though eavesdropping; she was changed, hopefully forever. Gray felt the words as much as he heard them; they brought cozy comfort, as though being tucked in, safe and warm.

She returned shortly dragging the large tarp. They worked to shove the ice onto the tarp and then pulled like draught horses to haul it back to the truck. There was just enough space to yank the tarp along one side of the trailer. Then, like whirling dervishes, they flung the ice into the trailer. Each suppressed the growing fear that any moment a Polar Oasis Search and Rescue truck would appear to "save" them. Finally, the last chunk was tossed in. Elisabeth was closest to the cabin, so Gray said, "You drive. I'll guide from back here." He walked behind the trailer, testing the firmness of the partially collapsed lava tube ceiling.

Elisabeth clambered up the cabin and then down the escape hatch. She didn't bother to pressurize the cabin and promptly engaged the motors. Checking the rear-facing camera, she saw Gray and the narrow channel. The truck's three-axis design, she hoped, would make it straightforward to thread this needle... or, at least, make it feasible.

"Take it slow" said Gray.

"Ha! Like I have a choice!"

The truck and trailer eased up the ramp, which appeared firm to Gray. Full faith was put in the vehicle designed for uncertain terrain. He gave guidance as Elisabeth deftly avoided collisions with the tube wall. The vehicle rolled back onto the surface to Gray's, "Fantastic!" Elisabeth added, "Easy peasy! I'll raise the antenna and ping Polar."

The payload of pure ice, perhaps worth millions of dollars, glistened in the sunlight that leaked over the horizon. Gray imagined what the scene would be like when this rolled into Malapert. He considered an equivalent sight a couple hundred years ago, if a wagon piled with gold had rolled into some 49er outpost. "Um, maybe we ought to cover the payload. Best not to attract too much attention." He turned to gingerly walk down the ramp to grab the tarp.

"Sounds good! I got through to Polar. They hadn't begun to worry yet. I said we took a route that was out of radio contact, which... is actually true."

———

Elisabeth took the drive to Malapert, careful to follow a path that avoided the line between the sun and Malapert Mountain. The lava tube was at the bottom of a basin illuminated by scant rays of sun, but the journey emerged onto a plain awash in light. Depending upon the route taken and availability of roads, it could be a one-hour or four-hour journey to the shimmering mountain. Their helmets had been removed for the trek.

The cabin brimmed with excitement. Elisabeth and Gray held hands and mused about imaginative escapes and futures that seemed bursting with possibilities. "What a team!" Elisabeth spontaneously cheered, to Gray's delight. They both sported smiles that might become permanent... assuming all went well.

Gray was on the lookout for posted signs that marked the boundary of the Mechanical Exclusivity Zone. Once back in the Zone, there would be a much better chance to find a road plus they'd have the advantage of navigation assistance with the repeaters.

"Bingo," said Gray, as he put down the scope to point in the distance. Elisabeth turned the truck toward the sign posted on a ridge. The truck drove up and along the crest toward the sign. As expected, it declared, "Leaving Lunar Open Zone / Entering Polar Oasis Ltd. Mechanical Exclusivity Zone."

"So far, so good," said Elisabeth. She tapped the navigation console. They were now within reach of the repeaters and their location was pinpointed, on the outskirts of the Haworth Crater region. The map highlighted a road to Malapert. She turned to intersect the road, which was just a beaten path, but it permitted her to pick up the speed. "Less than an hour to go!" she declared.

"Super... then what?" Having just brought their treasure to the domain of the robber barons, Gray lost his little smile.

"I've been thinking. Agents are licensed and bonded to record claims and pay the spot price. But..." she got a playful glint in her eye, "I've delivered countess loads to Assay Ops and worked with many agents. One agent stands out. Every time I work with this guy—his name is Slim—he tells me how tired he is of lunar duty. He wears a cowboy hat; I think he's from Texas. Anyway, he's always giving me updates about how he's been saving for years to return and... seriously... open a dude ranch. He has the ranch all planned out. It's posted on the wall in the office: Corral, barn, pasture, trails, everything."

"A dude ranch. What a cool idea."

"You don't get it, do you? We need to cut a deal with Slim. I think he can issue a temporary claim. He'd have to pay us spot price but in exchange for that claim we'd invest to help him buy that ranch. I think we can make this work."

Gray mulled this over. "Hmmm... You'll do the talking?"

"I'll do the talking."

"Then, easy peasy."

"As long as Slim is working today."

Malapert Mountain now dominated the sky to their left and the road turned straight for it, the sun safely on a different alignment. They soon rolled past "Welcome to Malapert Mountain Ops / Polar Oasis Ltd Mechanical Exclusivity Zone." Elisabeth slowed, because of what constituted traffic at the lunar south pole. There were even pedestrians. They were mostly Polar Oasis staff, mainly Scrapers who had delivered their loads of ore and were killing time to bill more hours. Almost all of them dreamed of striking it big. Almost all of them saw the trailer with a partially covered load of crystal-clear ice roll into the compound. But only one pair, Mort and Buzz, were independent prospectors who could file a spot claim from the field.

They jumped into their truck to backtrack along the new tire treads before the path was covered.

Mort guided the truck along the tread marks as he sped past startled pedestrians and cross-traffic. Buzz glanced up from his mobile and his toothpick bobbed as he spoke, "Nope. I just checked again. No new claims have been filed for over two months, not since Polar's last land grab. This is a new indie strike. Step on it!" Mort's gaze was fixed on the wide tread marks, which he could read as easily as a navigator roadmap. They exited the compound and he put the pedal to the metal, trailing huge flares of dust as they raced on their way toward the "Lunar Open Zone" sign.

Elisabeth turned toward Assay Ops, yet another giant tin foil igloo. She'd followed this process innumerable times hauling scraper ore. The truck eased alongside the igloo and into a fenced-in area until the trailer rested squarely on the weighing platform. "Helmet time," she said. They smiled and kissed as they exchanged helmets.

The cabin depressurized. "Just follow my lead; I'll do the talking, but if anyone asks, just agree with me." Gray nodded.

They stepped toward the entrance which had the same lavatory-style airlock as Haworth Ops, except, as Gray noted, "Hey, it's a 4-person airlock like Amundsen!" This time, Elisabeth could let the comment roll. On the outside was a notice, in bold red font: *Have your claim ready! New water only!* They entered the airlock and Elisabeth pointed through the interior window at the dude ranch map on the waiting room wall. Across the top of the map, in artful hand-drawn lettering, was "Golden Horseshoes Dude Ranch." She gave a grinning two thumbs-up. Then she heard a staticky click over the radio. Gray turned away and she heard him speak, "Oh, yeah, hi Paul... sorry, but I was off-line for a while." Laughter. "I'll have to call you back. I may have some news for our project." Pause. "No, she's cool, I mean... I'll explain later." He turned back to smile at Elisabeth. She looked away, as "ice queen" memories bubbled up. He found and held her hand and those memories floated away.

The airlock compression completed and they made their entrance, although nobody looked. The waiting area was empty; only one assay agent was behind the counter and it wasn't Slim. The agent was a middle-aged woman, looking no-nonsense as she held a document and squinted at fine print through the bottom of her bifocals. Elisabeth and Gray removed their helmets to the customary smell of bad office coffee and burnt gunpowder. Gray walked to the map as Elisabeth approached the woman, whose well-worn name tag read "Muriel."

"Hello, Muriel, I am Elisabeth Synder and I have a load to assay."

The agent, eyes still fixed on the document, extended her hand. "Claim."

"Is Slim here? He's a lot more familiar with some of the complexities of these claims."

44

"Slim hit the trail." Muriel finally made eye contact. "I am fully licensed and I've seen it all." She wiggled the fingers of the outstretched hand.

Many kilometers away, Buzz scanned the landscape with his scope. "Slow down... what's that?" He pointed to a path that stretched from the main road, across the open plain, and over the horizon, as if drawn with a sharp pencil. Mort slowly rolled the truck to carefully read the road. Buzz added, "Horizon's maybe 5 kliks from here. If the strike is just on the other side, we could be there inside of a half hour... we could score!"

Moments later, Mort stated, matter-of-fact: "Eureka." He turned the truck to follow the trail off the road. But Mort's flat voice belied his exultant expression. He exchanged high-fives with Buzz and the truck resumed its tear across the wide expanse.

In the Assay Office, Elisabeth had tested Muriel's patience to the breaking point when the airlock whooshed open. "Dang it! Got half way home and realized I forgot my hat!" Elisabeth turned to see Slim step into the office. He removed his helmet to reveal a mane of white hair, a fluffy white handlebar mustache, and a face weathered by country life. But when he saw Elisabeth, Slim's scowl turned into a beacon: "Why, if it isn't Miss Lizzy!"

Elisabeth rushed to give Slim a big hug, as Gray watched, flabbergasted. *Miss Lizzy?* Muriel peaked from behind her paper.

"Am I glad to see you!" Elisabeth gushed. "There's been a bit of a snafu... would you mind processing my claim?"

"There *is* no claim," said Muriel. "That's the *snafu*. Slim, you're off duty. I can handle..."

Slim raised his hand, and in a drawl as smooth as molasses, said, "Never you mind. I'll help Miss Lizzy, right after I get my hat." He walked behind the counter and put the brown cowboy hat on his head, while still wearing the rest of his pressure suit. "That way, I won't forget it. Now, what's the fuss?"

Elisabeth gestured for Slim to step to the far end of the counter, where, in a hushed voice, she explained the delicate situation. Muriel snapped back to her fine print and Gray returned to corrals, barns, and trails. After considerable back-and-forth, Slim said, in a voice loud enough for Muriel to hear, "Yep, I can grant a temporary claim, but I got to check the chemical fingerprint first. I've had clowns come in here with frozen tap water. Dumber than a bag of hammers. Or they scoop up ore from a Polar mine. The market is for *new* water." Then, sotto voce, "I know you know that, but..." he gave a discreet nod toward Muriel.

"No worries," whispered Elisabeth.

Slim stepped over to glance out the window at the trailer and gave a long whistle as he shook his head in disbelief. "Lord almighty. From the looks of it, y'all got yourselves quite a strike. And no claim. Anyone see your mine?"

"No; we didn't even see another truck until we rolled into Malapert."

"Good, but you can't never tell in these parts. Money makes a good man go crazy. That's one reason I want to hightail it back to West Texas. No money there!" He laughed. "Dump the ice in the chute. I'll run the test and compare to other claims. If there's no match, I'll issue the temporary claim."

Muriel, overhearing this, spoke up, "Can't do that. Need to wait 24 hours." Slim winked at Elisabeth and ignored Muriel.

Elisabeth knew the drill from her many scraper loads. Gray offered to help but she replied, "I got this part." She walked over to him, nodded toward the map, and whispered in his ear, "Learn everything you can about this, sweetheart. Let's make dreams come true." She punctuated it with a discreet kiss.

Elisabeth exited the dome, flung off the tarp, opened the chute's steel doors, and dumped in the load. Then she swung the doors shut and returned to the Assay Office. When she entered, she heard the familiar sound from underground of powerful pulverizers and grinding wheels. She walked over to the map to join Gray and, hopefully, lure Slim. Sure enough, Slim was irresistibly drawn and with open arms and broad smile, said, "What do y'all think?" as he walked over to join them. Gray opened up; his many dude ranch questions needed answers. This also opened the subject of dude ranch finances, for which the timing was perfect.

Mort blazed along the trail and slowed as the truck rolled up a bluff. Ahead, maybe a kilometer, was the lava tube pit, illuminated by the sun peeking over the ridge. It was surrounded by a scribble of tracks. "That's it!" shouted Buzz.

"Get out the sampler," said Mort, straining to stay cool. In minutes, the truck was at the pit. "I'll pop the antenna. Helmets on. Get ready to rock and roll."

Slim held court at Golden Horseshoes, gleefully taking Gray's questions and pointing to recent additions that perhaps Elisabeth hadn't yet noticed. Then the conversation meandered into speculations about investment financials. Meanwhile, beneath them, a slurry of lava tube ice was being melted.

Mort and Buzz bounded down the ramp, laughing, but they stopped before the gaping maw of the lava tube tunnel. "Jesus" said Buzz. They scanned the floor and walls with their flashlights, as far back as the curve, but no ice was visible, nor any evidence of digging. "How far back do you think they went?" Mort started with tentative steps but Buzz stopped, looking up at the uncertain ceiling. Just behind them, they entered down a section that seemed to have recently collapsed. But then, as greed overpowered fear, he picked up the pace and joined Mort.

Slim was enthralled by the prospect of an investment that could buy his freedom, but years of hoping had steeled him for disappointment. "I bought the land over ten years ago, but's it's still weeds and grass." With a dramatic sweep of his arm, he added, "But when I can put up all of this, well, then I'll be home free." He was lost in the carefully planned out dream.

Mort saw it first when his flashlight illuminated the deep chiseled-out ice pit. Even the loose pieces scattered about were worth thousands. "Holy shit. Get the sampler."

Buzz fumbled with unsteady hands but managed to unclip the sampler from his waist. It was bulky, with a small lid through which a sample would be dropped. Like a miniature version of the Assay Office analysis tool, the sampler would produce a fingerprint. More important, each sampler was certified and could submit a claim from the field.

Mort and Buzz raced back out of the tunnel and they scrambled up the ramp. As soon as they could see the truck's antenna, Mort shouted, "Transmit the claim!"

Buzz pressed the Transmit button, but a message displayed, "No satellite." He pressed again and again, cursing, "Damn it! Never a satellite when you need one! Shit!" Mort could only stare; he tried to cross his gloved fingers.

Suddenly, Slim glanced at a message on his wrist communicator. In a whisper, he said, "Hey, folks, the results are ready." Gray and Elisabeth pulled each other close. They reached to hold Slim but he turned away, seeing that Muriel had been watching, an eyebrow raised. Then he spoke up, officiously, "The chemical fingerprint analysis is complete. Let's see if there is a matching claim." They walked to the far end of the counter.

Elisabeth and Gray hovered behind Slim who was logged in and navigated a maze of pages, each of which painted more slowly than the last, or so it seemed. Finally, a fingerprint match page displayed: *No match.* The floodgates opened and they let up whoops as Slim waved his hat like a broncobuster. Gray and Elisabeth embraced with a long kiss, which made Slim burst into a hearty laugh. "Well, Miss Lizzy! It's about time!"

In the background was the sound of flapping paper. They turned to see Muriel wave a sheet of paper even more vigorously than Slim had waved his hat. "Sorry to spoil your party, but I just received a spot claim. Fingerprint matches yours. We need to check timestamps."

At the lava tube, Buzz and Mort danced an improvised jig and blew kisses skyward for LunaSat IV, as Mort cheered, "Now we just wait for the claim confirmation and then... we... will... be... *rich!*"

In the Assay Office, two printouts were laid side-by-side on the counter. With a red fingernail, Muriel pointed to the *Submission finish* line at the bottom of her sheet and tapped. "24 seconds before your finish." She sported a satisfied smile, the contented smile of someone who worshipped process, someone who worked for the process.

Slim, on the other hand, was someone who expected a process to work for him. He gently took her finger and moved it to the top of her form to *Submission start*, which was 33 minutes after the timestamp on his form. "We go by the start time. A spot checker processes a chip of sample; we just ground up over 3200 kilograms for this load. We want to be fair, don't we?"

Muriel looked back and forth at the forms before, with a little pout, she turned to Slim and said, "OK."

"Which one looks better, Miss Lizzy?" Gray tried on a white cowboy hat, waited, then tried on a tan cowboy hat.

Elisabeth turned around from the computer console. Behind her, gauzy curtains blew in the warm Mediterranean breeze. Through the window of their home above the Amalfi coastline, sailboats dotted the sea. "What did I say about calling me that?" Her wide grin made it hard for Gray to take her seriously, but she continued. "I'll answer your question, my love, but you have to answer one for me."

"Deal."

"OK, first I like the tan hat. White hats are for good guys." Gray tilted his head, as she added, "OK, now my question." Her face scrunched up, as if it was hard to ask, "What did you talk about on Channel C?"

Gray tossed aside the white hat while he shifted gears. It had been a while since he thought about Channel C. "Oh... well, I had a project with a friend."

"Really? What?" She sat upright, hands folded, ready for anything.

"It's ancient history now." He could see that she wasn't going to relent, so, with a sigh he said, "We wanted to open a coffeeshop at Amundsen base." Elisabeth had braced for the outrageous, so when she heard this, she relaxed back into the chair. "It would have donuts and other pastries. But really good coffee. We thought if we did it first, you know, mechanical exclusivity, we could lock up the market and make a good living. All of those Scrapers and Prospectors coming in from the field, you know." He looked sheepish. "Kind of anticlimactic now, I guess."

She could only nod as she processed this. "No reason to be embarrassed." After collecting herself, she gestured to the computer screen behind her. "Speaking of booming lunar business prospects, we just got the best-and-final offer from Polar for our claim. The robber barons would double the amount of the original truckload. So, either we take their offer or we go back to the Moon and dig in, so to speak. Do you want to operate a lunar ice mine?"

"Let me think about that: No," came the brisk reply, as Gray focused on his luggage.

"Done." She swiveled back to the computer to accept the robber barons' terms.

Gray carefully situated the tan hat in the suitcase, packing so that it would stay in shape on the long flight to El Paso. Then, for the hundredth time, he reviewed the activity schedule for their stay at Golden Horseshoes Dude Ranch. "I was worried that I'd be too jet lagged for the roping class, but I think the sunshine will keep me awake. Stay clear, though; I might rope you by mistake."

Elisabeth attended to her packing and smiled. "Worse things could happen."

ALPHA
AND OMEGA

T HE BEDROOM NEXT to Sam's was empty at last. It was blissfully
quiet, too; his father's coughing would never again echo through
the claustrophobic Brooklyn apartment. The last gasps brought
satisfying closure to Sam. Mission accomplished. But a loud voice in
Sam's head expressed another opinion:

"You killed him!" charged Little Sam.
Big Sam would have none of it. "He was tired and
ready to go. He hated me and I hated him right back. Now
it's time to move on and out of here."

Sam set a large cardboard box in front of his dresser. The box was
empty, top open, bottom taped, ready to be stuffed. The cheap dresser
was covered by a shiny veneer, a woodgrain print worn away by years
of grabby fingers. It had unbonded along the corners and seams and
was repaired with tape. When he first used the dresser, it was too high
to reach the top drawer. He'd drag a cherry red child-size chair across
the matted carpet and carefully balance as he plucked Spider-Man
underwear and Batman socks. Those were the sunny times before the
spreading desolation after Mom's death darkened the world. In those
halcyon days, the only voice in Sam's head was Little Sam.

Sam put a layer of clothes into the box. Then he picked up a framed photograph from the dresser top and held it tenderly. It was a 4 x 6-inch color print of a laughing young woman, but part of the photo was torn away. The picture was mounted in a tired gilt frame, smudged with fingerprints from frequent handling. The woman was the mother he didn't remember. The missing piece had been ripped out by Big Sam. It was his father.

> Little Sam tried to summon an air of authority to counter the belligerence. "He was a good man. To switch his meds with placebos was murder."
>
> Big Sam had the twisted malevolence to make light of anything. "Placebos never killed anyone!" And he had the instinct to rationalize anything. "I didn't make him drink booze for the last 20 years after Mom died."
>
> "You're crazy to blame him for Mom's death."
>
> "I don't blame him for that. I blame him for not filling the gap, then becoming a boozer. He abandoned us."
>
> It was familiar territory and they were on the same downward spiral. Little Sam would fight the good fight but it was like pushing a giant boulder uphill, the accretion of a lifetime of Big Sam's hate. Now, Big Sam had triumphed over the father and Little Sam was squelched, too, as the boulder of hate forced him into the depths of Sam's ugly and malignant mind.

Sam kissed the picture and gently rested it on the clothes in the box. Then he turned to the task at hand and layered on the remaining top-drawer contents. The box was sealed and he proceeded to the other drawers and boxes until the dresser was packed.

He progressed through the bedroom. His pale, wiry frame moved smoothly, deftly picking and choosing what to pack and what to throw away. This had been his room for all of his 20 years. Combing through possessions was an archeological exercise. But, with Little Sam quiet, Big Sam made all of the decisions and the job was quickly completed. Childhood treasures were gathered in one box, an old steel toy dump truck, an unopened Play-Doh container, and Lego treasures. The rest of the apartment's contents, his father's lifetime possessions, would be liquidated.

Sam took a folded paper from his pocket and opened it. He'd leased a room in the new apartment from another young man named Jim, who had posted the ad where Sam worked, on the Brooklyn Energy internal website. Big Sam had turned on the charm during the interview and scored. Now it was time for the move, a few blocks and a world away.

Sam looked at the phone number on the paper and texted, "Yo Jim! I'll be there at about four."

"Great!" came Jim's reply.

Across town, Jim packed for his move.

His mother watched from his bed. She dabbed reddened eyes with a lace handkerchief; a diamond bracelet caught the light. "I know this is the right thing, but I feel awful."

Jim turned from the box to gesture out the floor-to-ceiling window. "It's about time, and I'll just be across the river." She looked through forlorn tears at the urban panorama beneath a cloudless afternoon sky. Fate had given Jim an unobstructed view of his new Brooklyn neighborhood, or at least its environs, from the family's Manhattan high-rise condominium. Pointing, he added, "I'll be somewhere over there. It'll be fun for you to visit after I scout around and find places to show." He put his arms around her.

Her adoring eyes gazed at him but then glanced away. "I'm sure your father would like to come, too." It was a risky comment.

Jim broke the embrace and returned to packing, now with a vengeance. "He'd be disappointed. I'd rather that he stay away." The box was full and he shoved it aside to move onto the next as his mother sobbed. He snatched an armload of drawer contents and stuffed them into the box. "I mean, I think he'll be relieved that I am gone. Just like I think he's glad I quit the company to take the new job."

"You *know* that's not true. He was so proud when you started at Brooklyn Energy and…"

"Right, when I *started*. When he thought I'd be a star employee." He yanked open the bottom drawer and slung clothes into the last box. "When he thought I'd hit my numbers so he could impress his executive buddies. Before I blew it." He slammed the empty drawer shut and manhandled the box flaps, tearing one. "Shit!" His mother openly cried and rushed out of the room.

"It'll be fine!" he shouted. "I already have a roommate! I'll make friends and start a life, *my life*, over there." He stacked the boxes onto the dolly. "And working at the health food store will be a hell of a lot less stress than being an S.O.B. at Brooklyn Energy."

She returned to the doorway, composed. "S.O.B.?"

"Son of boss, or, in my case, son of boss' boss' boss… I lost count, but it doesn't matter now. Thank God!"

She wanted to change the topic. "Who's your roommate?"

"It's a guy named Sam… also works at Brooklyn Energy. I posted the listing there before I left. Seems like a good guy." The news injected a badly needed dose of hope. They smiled and embraced. "He'll be at the apartment soon; I need to head out."

He kissed her forehead; she sighed as the door closed behind him.

━━━━━━━

The scene in the apartment lobby was a happy coincidence, as they both arrived at about the same time.

"Hey, you look familiar!" joked Jim.

Sam smiled. "Well, there goes the neighborhood!" which triggered a good-natured laugh from Jim.

Two young men, dollies stacked with boxes, steered toward the elevator as much as toward a future budding with optimism. Jim pressed the *Down* button. "I've got to drop a box off in the storage locker. You got anything to store?"

Sam thought about the box of childhood artifacts that, on reflection, he was ready to put away. "Sure."

The locker side trip was uneventful. An empty cage was unlocked, two boxes were shoved in, and the cage was locked. Jim pulled a key off his keychain. "This is your locker key."

They rolled their payloads to the elevator. Sam pushed the "4" and looked to Jim for confirmation which came with a nod. Minutes later, the door opened onto the 4th floor and Jim took the lead, just a couple of steps to the apartment across the hall. "Close to transportation!"

"Commuter friendly," added Sam. "So… we didn't discuss this at our little interview, but what do you do at B.E.?"

Jim unlocked the apartment and swung the door open. He backed in with his dolly. "Not there anymore. I posted the listing on my final day, which was last week."

Sam followed into the apartment and the door closed. He was puzzled by the reply. "What happened?"

Jim rolled the dolly into his room and kept the conversation going. "My dad's a VP there. Kind of helped me get the job. Big mistake. BIG. It sucked being an S.O.B."

Sam started to unbox in his room. "So, was it just the S.O.B. thing, you know, others giving you a hard time? Or was your dad a jerk about it, too?"

"It was *only* my dad being a jerk. It was the last nail in the coffin. My dad and I don't get along and this move will finally separate us. I'd be fine never seeing him again."

The comment tickled Big Sam. Another soul victimized by a toxic father. A new and special friend?

Little Sam was distracted by the box in the locker, forgotten treasures in the basement.

Jim shifted gears. "So, what do you do? It's a good company, you know, otherwise."

Sam was still fixated on the S.O.B. comment but dislodged himself to reply, "I'm in Quality Assurance." The dry topic stifled the conversation, but there was unpacking and shopping to do and plenty of other conversations to have. It would be a full day.

The apartment settling proceeded smoothly, collaboratively. The day wound down as they each neared exhaustion.

Several months earlier and 750 million kilometers from Brooklyn, volcanoes on Jupiter's moon Io disgorged geysers of lava. Streamers glowed orange along graceful plumes in the near vacuum until the molten ejecta splashed onto Io's mottled surface. Spattered lava almost instantly froze to glassy stone, except for rare scarlet pools that stubbornly refused to cool. These sparsely scattered deposits contained Q, an intensely radioactive material that generated its own heat, fierce and seemingly limitless.

Over the dark and frozen landscape lumbered autonomous vehicles shaped like huge tortoises whose shells protected them from the hellish rain. The machines searched for pools of Q and scooped the contents into ceramic bellies. The tortoise robots then transported their superheated payload to refinery intakes.

After Q was dumped into an intake pipe, the automated refinery performed the alchemy of Polar Division. This neutralized Q into its complimentary forms of Q-alpha and Q-omega, each inert when kept apart. The refining process involved a high-speed centrifuge that separated the still-molten material and shunted alpha and omega out along diametrically opposed pipelines before the substances cooled, which completed the division. By this time, the inert Q-alpha and Q-omega were over ten meters apart. The distance was critical. It was too distant for the two constituents to exert the irresistible mutual pull that would draw them together and trigger the violent return to molten, radioactive Q.

Along separate packaging systems, an endless row of small steel vials was each filled with 30 grams of material. The vials were bunched into payloads of Q-alpha or Q-omega, to be launched via railgun toward Earth. The inert payloads, alternately one type and then the other, were captured months later near Earth for ultimate delivery to Brooklyn Energy

The weekly shipment of Q arrived at Brooklyn Energy. It was Q-omega, as expected, because last week's shipment was Q-alpha. Parallel receiving systems handled the incoming deliveries. It wasn't practical to scrub and reuse the same equipment between batches, for even dust from the two constituents would snap together and flare into a scorching radioactive flash if brought close enough.

Sam had been on the QA job in Payload Receiving for six months and mastered the procedures. He decided that they were idiot-proof and the "separate but equal" material handling made the worst accidents impossible. The staff only came in contact with the material through heavy rubber gloves built into containment chambers.

Sam's primary job was to draw random samples from the steel vials to conduct purity tests. Calibration of the automated refinery on Io tended to drift in the hostile environment. Impurities reduced the alpha + omega energy yield and resulted in waste. To mix 95% pure alpha with 99% pure omega would waste 4% of the omega. So, the trick to optimal energy generation was to mix materials of equivalent purity.

Invariably, the handling and the purity tests resulted in small amounts of waste. Disposal procedures were clear, but Sam spied loopholes, that is, if one was determined to liberate a pinch of alpha or omega. He learned in safety training that the separated material was so benign that there were reports of people inhaling and even ingesting the inert dust in accidents with no ill effects. Q was like lead and would bind to bone. Small amounts would not cause health problems. But, if someone with alpha or omega poisoning ever came near the counterpart constituent then their lives would end in a fiery and radioactive finale. The training ended with this lesson to instill self-preserving caution.

The final safety lesson had fascinated Big Sam. Today, he thought about it as he pondered his new friend and his toxic father. Poor Jim. *Jim said he'd be fine never to see his father again.*

The next few days of tests left rust-colored Q-omega dust on Sam's gloves; also, carefully choreographed sloppiness caused minor spillage. The loose material, about 15 grams worth, was discretely gathered and sequestered in a spare glass vial tucked in a corner of the containment chamber. During a supervisor rotation, Sam deftly opened the chamber to reach in and slip the sealed glass vial into his pocket.

At the end of the day, he strode out of Payload Receiving without raising a scintilla of suspicion. Once back at the apartment, the vial was stored in his basement locker box.

> "One down, one to go!" cheered Big Sam, "And then just wait! The chance will come to expose Jim's father to the alpha and omega."
>
> "I can't let you get away with this," came Little Sam's voice, faint and remote as if from the bottom of a well.
>
> Big Sam, undeterred, continued, "Collateral damage should be minimized, but to make an omelet you have to break a few eggs."

The following week, the larceny was repeated for Q-alpha, this time with a spare steel vial that wouldn't be missed. However, it occurred to Sam that a switch was needed to keep the purple alpha dust safely separated from the omega as he carried it into the building. While the apartment was on the 4th floor, certainly far enough from the basement locker, the path through the lobby passed too near the basement sample. So, before leaving for work on the morning of the theft, Sam retrieved the Q-omega from the locker. He brought it to the apartment, wrapped it in clothing, and wedged it safely in a drawer.

At the end of the day, the stolen Q-alpha was safely carried through the lobby to the elevator. The vial was then stashed in the box on the locker floor, pressed into a freshly opened can of childhood Play-Doh.

Days turned into weeks that turned into months, until one rainy autumn morning. Sam awoke to the sound of Jim pacing back and forth in the living room, repeatedly hitting a floorboard squeak. In the blustery morning, rain whacked against the window. Over this, Sam clearly heard, "Shit… shit… shit…" almost as a mantra. It was time for work anyway, so he got up to investigate.

"Hey, good morning… what's up?"

"My dad. I just saw that he emailed me late yesterday. He's going to stop by tonight… wants to 'mend fences'."

Sam's head cleared as he woke up. "Oh. Can't you just tell him not to come?"

Jim stopped in his tracks to stare at Sam. "You're kidding, right?" Sam had no reaction. Jim explained, shaking a fist with each new point. "You don't know my dad. Ex-Marine. Type A executive. Once he's made up his mind, it… it's futile." Then he returned to pacing and the "shit" mantra.

Big Sam saw his opportunity. The trap could be set.

Sam cleared his throat. "I could stay here and you could stay… out. Then, you know, I could maybe hang out with your dad and ping you when he's finally given up and left." Jim considered this, and Sam added, "Seriously, it's no problem. I'm not going anywhere in this weather anyway. After your shift at the health food store, you can chill… across the street at Donut Nut!" He laughed at his own suggestion.

Jim chuckled, too. He wasn't passive aggressive, but if he would ever… *ever*… 'mend fences' it would be on his terms. He looked at Sam, "Sure. Thanks, man. He said he's coming by at six to take me out for dinner. Just tell him something came up." The rain came down in sheets, obscuring even the building across the street. "And he'll be here, come hell or high water."

"No problemo. Does he like coffee or tea?"

"Coffee."

Little Sam shouted, "No, you don't!"

61

"Didn't you ever get tired of bending to Dad's will? Don't you wish someone had done this for us?"

"I'd rather mend fences than burn them!"

"And look where that got you. I'm going to do for Jim what someone should have done for us years ago. Jim's dad will have a special cup of coffee; he won't even know. Then… and I'm thinking how best to do this… perhaps he will get a letter at the office. Flame mail!"

"And you'll incinerate any witnesses…"

"Right; all utterly untraceable. It will be chalked up as an industrial accident involving mishandling of Q. And I will be here to comfort Jim, my special buddy."

Jim dressed and left, shrouded in a poncho, with a thumbs-up on the way out.

Sam wasn't far behind. The machinations of the epochal day began to move into place.

Promptly at 6:00pm there was a crisp rap at the door. Sam had the serenity of a person confident of their journey and destination. He rose from the sofa, feeling the glass vial of Q-omega in his shirt pocket that until recently had been stowed in the dresser drawer. He opened the door and stood before a massive and solid man built like a grizzly bear. His trench coat was soaked from the rain that dripped from short-cropped gray hair and along a face that appeared to have had its smile muscles removed.

"You must be Jim's father! Come in!" gushed Sam, willing himself to be effusive.

"Thank you," came the perfunctory reply in a barrel-chested baritone. "I am Rex Willoughby. Where is my son?" He looked down at Sam with cold, blue-gray eyes.

"I'm Sam. Take off that wet coat. It's still really coming down! I have some coffee brewing. Would you like some?"

Rex eyed Sam skeptically as he removed the coat and handed it over. "Where's Jim?"

"Jim… had to work late and run some errands. He sends his regrets. He won't be able to join you tonight." Sam showed Rex to the dining table.

Rex planted his bulk in the chair and appeared unconvinced. He rested his folded hands on the table. Even the fingers looked muscular.

"Coffee?" asked Sam, a slight quaver slipping in. He didn't want to prepare the concoction if it wouldn't be drunk.

"Enough with the coffee. I expect Jim to be here." He barked the words as if admonishing a subordinate who failed a minor task.

Sam took a step back as if shoved by the words. "Yes, well, like I said, he sends his regrets. Perhaps you would like to arrange to come by tomorrow?" The conversation strained Big Sam's cunning. To manipulate his own father was child's play compared to this beast.

Jim had been killing time at Donut Nut, having made his way over after his shift at the health food store, as planned. He ordered a plain donut because he was hungry; the first donut he'd had in years. He took a bite and decided it *might* have been fresh much earlier that day. As he held this foreign food, he considered the odd situation. Sitting in this place, parka dripping, cold, hungry. Through the sheets of rain, he could see his apartment lobby, water streaming down the street like a small river. His father would have passed through there minutes ago.

The months since leaving home gave Jim perspective. Growing up, so much of what he did was a reaction to his father instead of something thoughtful and deliberate. What he'd studied in school and even his hobbies had been shaped by his overpowering father. He'd taken the job at Brooklyn Energy at his father's urging. Then, when he'd failed at his first assignment, he ran away like a little boy, still frightened of disapproval.

It all felt juvenile, as if he couldn't trust his own judgement, his moral compass. Sitting at Donut Nut was a reaction. And the stale donut was awful. It was time to grow up and own what came next.

At last, Jim saw his moral compass point true. It pointed across the street.

He stood and marched out into the rain, casting the donut in the garbage. He leapt over the gutter stream and charged across the street as rain pelted him like bullets against Godzilla. He leapt across the other gutter stream, across the sidewalk, and into the apartment lobby. He knew his dad would still be there. He had played this waiting game before.

Jim removed the parka and shook it off in the entryway where he saw a hastily written sign taped to the wall: "Basement flooded. Clear your locker ASAP."

"Shit." He took a deep breath and exhaled. This had to be done now before the water rose further. It was only two boxes.

Upstairs, Rex wasn't budging. The coffee offers stopped. Chiseling small talk had exposed an interesting fact. With a laser-like stare, Rex said, "So, you work at Brooklyn Energy." Sam felt like a wildebeest who had stepped too close to a watering hole. The crocodile had struck.

"Um, yes, I work in Quality Assurance." He fidgeted and stuttered. "P-Payload Receiving."

"Rasmussen's organization." With an icy gaze, Rex added, "She's good but she's got some *real clowns* on her team."

This plan was going nowhere, and Sam just wanted to put the vial back and try again some other time. He wanted to escape from this diamond anvil of a human being.

At that moment, the elevator arrived and its door opened across the hall, with Jim and the boxes.

Sam shrieked and clutched his chest as the vial shattered and glass fragments tore into his flesh. He was yanked backward, scarcely able to maintain his balance as he fought against the violent force. Rex lurched to help, thinking Sam was having a heart attack. But a growing circle of blood on Sam's chest suddenly made clear that something else was happening. The ex-Marine had heard no gun shot and he used his full strength to stop Sam's surge back toward an invisible spot behind the kitchen wall.

From the water-soaked box in Jim's arms, a container of yellow Play-Doh had burst out, rocketed across the hall, and slammed into the wall. Jim dropped the boxes in the hall, stunned. From inside the apartment, he heard his father yell, "Fight it, Sam! Stay strong!" Jim's body shook as he fumbled in his pocket for the key ring. He retrieved the apartment key and struggled to slide it into the lock, spellbound by the deepening Play-Doh crater.

The door swung open and Jim raced to his father and Sam, who was drifting in and out of consciousness. The Q-omega, and the glass shards it stuck to, drove relentlessly through muscle, bone, and blood vessels toward the Q-alpha in the hallway. He was critically hemorrhaging.

"Call 9-1-1!" shouted Rex. Jim made the call.

Big Sam was incredulous as his world collapsed, like a high stakes gambler who had wagered everything and lost. The currency of hatred and manipulation was utterly devalued. He was broke. He was broken.

And then, in what remained of Sam's malignant mind, Big Sam was no more.

Little Sam, Sam's first and only voice so many years ago, still remained to the end. And he wanted to do whatever was possible to limit any harm to innocents.

Sam coughed and took a breath. "It's Q... it's Q..."
Rex was shocked. Jim, on the call, relayed the crucial fact to the emergency responders.
Sam continued, as he hacked up blood and looked down at the crimson crater in his chest. "That's omega... and outside... is alpha. 15 grams each..." Then his eyes closed and he was silent.

Rex bearhugged Sam to slow his advance toward the Q-alpha and the radioactive fireball that would result. Jim ended the call and shouted as he went out the open door, "I know where the alpha is!"

In the hallway, Jim dug away the yellow Play-Doh to reveal the end of the steel vial, which had remained intact. It was embedded in an aluminum drywall brace, its ceaseless advance slowed but not stopped.

"Jim!" shouted his father, sounding winded. "Hurry! I'm losing the battle!"

Jim tore open his storage box to look for anything that could help. He found a miniature pair of pliers from a boyhood tool belt. Sam's soggy shredded box contained mainly toys. He grabbed a toy truck and turned back to the crater. With the pliers, he gripped the vial of Q-alpha, careful not to strain it while his hands trembled. He slowly and gingerly twisted and loosened the vial. Then he reached down for the stout metal dump truck. He placed the wheels against the wall and held it with one hand while he finished the vial extraction with the other. Fighting against the Q force to hold the vial, he wheeled the truck against the wall and eased the vial into the truck's bed, where the force of attraction made a small dent and kept the vial in place. Jim's heart pounded so hard he felt it in the fingertips that pressed against the truck.

The truck's stiff little tires bit into the wall. He pushed the truck along the wall and closely watched to ensure the vial stayed wedged against the bed. Tread marks embossed the wall and became shallower as the truck rolled away from the Q-omega that now changed course as it tore through Sam's lifeless body.

After several meters along the wall, the tread marks disappeared and the force of gravity overtook the Q force. The vial loosened; with an innocuous "clink", the cataclysmic material harmlessly dropped. Jim righted the truck and the vial rolled in the bed as he carried it to the far end of the hall.

He collapsed and sat on the floor next to the truck. The struggle against the Q force ended, Jim saw his father step out of the apartment and look for him. Rex's front was soaked with Sam's blood. Jim was too spent to call out and also too spent to worry about how his father might judge him, even now. But, more than ever, that didn't matter: He had the confidence of his moral compass.

As Rex rushed toward his son, the mysterious tracks along the wall caught his attention and he paused, then he saw the toy dump truck next to Jim… and, as he neared, he saw the vial in the truck.

Recognition dawned.

Rex kneeled next to Jim. He firmly gripped his son's shoulders and looked into his eyes, eyes that showed quiet confidence. "I cannot imagine a prouder father." The giant man was changed. From that moment, he also saw Jim as giant. They stood; he wanted to hold his son, but not against the bloody shirt. They shook hands and Rex planted a tender kiss on his son's forehead. And against the cacophony of first responders that streamed into the hallway, Jim embraced his father.

KRAKEN ENCOUNTER

BENEATH TITAN'S UMBER sky, beneath a hundred meters of liquid methane in the Kraken Mare, the *Nemo* cruised on its first deep dive. We were the intrepid explorers, Sarah and I, packed into the submersible, barely able to sit and stand. After the first uneventful hour, we began to feel tenuous confidence when the sub lurched to a halt and was whacked by a pickaxe, or that's what it sounded like. As we gathered our wits, we stared at each other, mute as our ears rang. But I knew what she was thinking because I was thinking it, too. She was captain and I was science lead, but after innumerable emergency drills we were a team.

As the ringing diminished, it was replaced by shrill alarms, each demanding attention. The submarine still had power, and through the dim red light we instinctively checked for leaks, which fortunately was negative. Sarah's brow furrowed, and she bit her lip as she grappled with the telemetry and alarms. I slowly shone the flashlight across the interior hull to assess integrity. Then I saw it: A deep crease, near the bow. "Sarah," I said, fixing the light on the crease. We were both on autopilot, following protocol. But I could tell from Sarah's reaction that she'd had no simulation for this. "What... the... hell...?" was all she could offer.

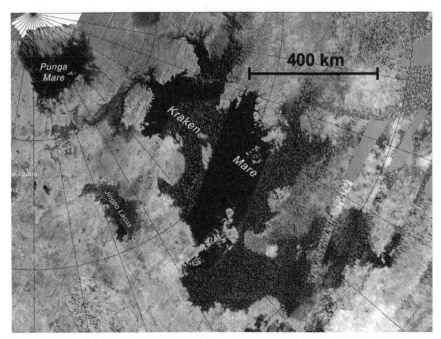

Kraken Mare in the Northern Hemisphere of Titan (credit: NASA)

She slowly shook her head and turned back to the navigation dashboard. The yellow and red indicators cast a burnt orange glow on her face, now showing perspiration. "We aren't moving," she said, "I don't get it. All four propellers are spinning, but... double-checking... the attitude control system swung them down. They are aiming *down* to keep the vessel level; the aft screws are turning a lot faster than the fore." The large internal combustion engine that powered the four directional propellers—two fore and two aft—had functioned well, fueled by external tanks filled with liquid oxygen that mixed with the sea's freely available liquid methane. When the *Nemo* cruised, their horizontal thrust, coupled with the hydroplanes that acted like wings, maintained the sub's depth and attitude.

"What about the other instruments?" I asked, but I only was groping, as much in the dark as the *Nemo*. As science lead, I knew emergency procedures, but I lacked Sarah's mastery and there always seemed to be multiple ways to deduce the status of this remarkable vessel.

She interrogated the console, reporting what she saw, talking more to herself than to me. "All instrumentation is intact. It all says the same thing: We are stuck and…" she tapped a blood red rectangle, "… Nemo isn't happy about this."

"We must have plowed into something to have caused *that*," I said, gesturing with my thumb at the crease behind me. The alarms had timed out, one by one, or been shut off by Sarah so that we could think clearly again. But in addition to the throaty beat of the engine and the whirring propellers there was a new sound, a sound that didn't belong. Something *outside* was dragging across the hull, around the bow. It was irregular, persistent, and disturbing. The sound scraped our nerves as we strained to focus on the telemetry to understand what was happening.

"Forward sonar shows clear sailing; nothing ahead. We are about fifteen meters from the sea floor, *but stuck here*," she repeated, now shaking her head as a drop of sweat fell onto the console between her clenched fists. Then she tapped a sequence into the control panel and the engine and propeller noise stopped. "Let's see if we fall." The aft slowly dropped, pivoting around the stationary bow. We had to shift our footing and reorient to keep from tumbling into each other. She restarted the engine, which rumbled to life, and the whirring propellers did their job, restoring the horizontal attitude. She looked up briefly to follow the path of the dragging sound before returning to the task at hand.

Sarah muttered to herself and shook her head again, sweat flying off, which was more troubling than any alarm. She had piloted the *Nemo* on the inaugural and the several subsequent surface and submersible sea trials. I was also science lead on those, but they were conducted in shallower depths, close to shore. Those tests polished Sarah's piloting skills and gave us the confidence for this first deep dive. But that confidence was nearing a breaking point.

I turned to Sarah. "Let's take a look outside." There was no ambient light at this depth, but the *Nemo* had cameras and lights mounted on its hull. These were intended for investigations near the sea floor and had been turned off during our submerged cruise. I turned on Bow Camera 2, which was mounted near the crease. The monitor flickered to life and showed an out-of-focus view of rivets on the hull because the camera was in its stowed position for safety. Sarah looked over my shoulder as I grabbed the articulator and twisted my wrist to swing the camera and its light up and away from the hull, punching a cone of Earthling light into the deep blackness.

The sight that swept into view caused my hand to shake. I released the articulator that remained pointed into the open sea. The hull with its crease cut a bright arc across the bottom of the monitor, but above and extending into the darkness was an array of fine crisscrossed lines.

Sarah said it first: "It's a web."

Something twitched at the top-right corner of the monitor. Sarah pointed to a place off-monitor and I grabbed the articulator again to point in that direction. Then, for an instant, we saw something huge and disorienting, a wildly out-of-scale insect or arachnid, larger than a human. I held my breath as my hair stood on end and fingertips tingled. But after a fleeting glance it scrambled away. It was at least a couple of meters long, and its frenzied legs moved with freakish dexterity and speed. Then, from the fringe of illumination, it abruptly stopped and turned back, briefly presenting a cigar-shaped profile. From the faint scattered light, we could see shadowy legs. Five? Ten? Each spindly appendage had jointed limbs perhaps a meter long. Most of the limbs gripped the web, but three slowly drifted, almost aimless. Legs? Arms? Antennae to feel vibrations or maybe to taste us? Penetrating the darkness, even from that distance, were five disks that glowed in reflected light: Eyes. Each independently shifted back and forth, up and down, to study the *Nemo*, its prey. Three glared as wide as the eyes of deep-sea squids and glowed blue-green in reflected light like those of the nocturnal animals on Earth. The other two were half as large and glowed orange-red.

"The eyes see in multiple spectra," I deduced.

"Sizing us up," said Sarah.

I turned the camera and zoomed out to survey the damage around the crease. "That's not good," breathed Sarah. The bow of the *Nemo* was tightly wrapped within webbing. Her voice quavered, "the scraping... like what a snared fly would hear." We had interrupted our entombment, temporarily.

I swung around the camera to look for the creature. It was upon us! Details were brought into crisp focus. It gripped the cocoon woven around the bow, eye cluster fixed on the crease. Its black body was covered by a thick stubble of white hair-like stalks that cast strong shadows in the spotlight. Beneath the forest of stalks, shiny leathery hide twitched like horseflesh drawn tight over angular skeletal contours. Slots behind the head were lined with thin folds of gray-green flesh, rhythmically pulsing, reminiscent of gills.

Then a shiny yellow bump formed beneath the eye cluster. The bump grew like a finger pressing out from the interior and the protruding flesh adopted a translucent crystalline appearance as it lengthened. It extended to at least half a meter and tapered to a sharp point. I watched, delirious with fascination, as this menacing icepick was poised to deliver a death puncture. Sarah shoved me aside and jerked the spotlight, swinging it while extending the boom to which it was mounted. She swept it toward the spike, but the creature spun around and retreated again, although not as far as before. Its weapon remained deployed, framed by flickering eyes.

Sarah grabbed my shoulders, her face inches from mine, and shouted, "What the hell were you thinking? We have to kill that thing, or we'll never get out of here!"

"We didn't come here to kill," was all I could stammer, as survival instincts wrestled with overpowering curiosity.

With a withering look of disgust, she turned to the command panel as she pointed toward the articulator. "Use that to keep it away," she ordered. "Buy us some time. I need to think."

I fixed the light and camera on the creature. It would abruptly shift away from the beam, but I swiveled my wrist to track it, keeping it at bay before it could rush us. While engaged in this cat and mouse encounter, I pondered how to classify its taxonomy. This important matter was properly suited for serious consideration in Titan's umber-colored light of day. But, studying its shadowy form, I decided on a working label: "*Arachnida titania*," I declared, to no comment from Sarah. She gave a quick glance toward my monitor to ensure I was still on task.

Moments later, she emerged from the analysis. She straightened and stretched, as much as the confined space permitted. I turned to her, but she promptly gestured for me to return to the monitor. I noticed that the sweat was gone. Then she spoke, "I am going to throw us into reverse and maybe, god willing, the web will slide off the tapered bow and we'll be free of it."

"And if we aren't? If we are snagged?"

"Our options are…" she paused to take a deep breath, "…*very* limited. We have the sample arm in the belly and it would make a mean weapon with the drill deployed. We could maybe gut the thing, but we'd have to swing the sub into the beast, somehow."

The violent image repulsed me.

"What about the external liquid oxygen tanks?" While minding the monitor, I gestured in the general direction of the valves used to fill and discharge the two tanks. "Could the discharge be aimed?"

"Our fuel? LOX will just sink; it's twice as dense as the liquid methane. But it's an idea, if we can… no… I can't see how we can chance it. That's our ticket back to base. We have a reserve, but even if we were lucky, I don't think it would kill the beast."

"But, why kill it?" I said, flipping my wrist to follow A. Titania's moves. She was clever, trying new dance steps to outsmart the light, to outsmart me.

"Is that a trick question?", she snapped. "If we can't escape, that thing will breach the hull at the first chance it gets. So, you better stay on point. I'm throwing the boat into reverse. Grab onto something." I couldn't bear the thought that A. Titania's life might hang by a thread, by a strand of web that could prevent our escape.

After a short patter of screen taps, the *Nemo* shuddered as the engine roared to a high RPM, almost masking the high-pitched whine from the four propellers now thrusting away from the web.

A. Titania watched the scene from her lair, pinned by the floodlight. As the *Nemo* pulled to escape, the light illuminated the web as it stretched. The *Nemo's* mounting surges fought my attempt to keep the light fixed on her, and as the cone of light swept, it caught glimpses of her in stroboscopic flashes, each exposing her frantic rush toward the *Nemo* along the lengthening trunk line, spike shining, eyes staring ahead, staring squarely at me. Then the camera violently slammed into the hull with a bang as our retreat was abruptly stopped. "I can't move the camera!" I shouted.

Sarah hollered over the noise, "The web snagged it. Turn on Aft Camera 1. I'm deploying the sample arm and spinning up the drill. Get ready for twist and shout!"

"No!" I shouted. I leapt in front of Sarah toward a discharge valve. She tried to push me away, but the churning sub worked in my favor and I fully twisted the valve, dumping a tank of liquid oxygen. Sarah punched me in the stomach and I fell back, but a sudden explosion from outside belted both of us senseless.

———

I awoke first and into a cacophony of alarms, the roaring engine, and the whining propellers. The sub heaved as the propellers fought to stabilize it. In the tumult, Sarah had been flung into her chair and lay unconscious, arms and legs splayed. I checked and found a strong pulse. Then my thoughts turned to A. Titania. Holding tight as the cabin pitched, I turned to the monitor. It still displayed the live feed from Aft Camera 1 that I had flipped on just before the explosion. I started a sweep with the camera, as best I could from the unsteady vessel.

From behind, I could hear Sarah groan, "Ugh… you and your idiotic LOX attack. You almost blew us to smithereens." She gingerly positioned herself in front of the control panel, wincing. "Any spark would have done the trick." She tapped into the panel. "The LOX probably came in contact with the busted Bow Camera 2. Add liquid methane and it's the Fourth of July."

I concentrated on my task.

Sarah continued tapping, the engine's roar softened, and the propellers faded into the background as the vessel stabilized. Alarms were silenced. With ice-cold sarcasm, she added, "I *do* hope your cute friend is safe and sound."

I ignored the sentiment. "I don't know." I hadn't seen the web yet but then a long rope-like filament swept into view, its loose end flailing. "Here's something", I said, zooming in on the end and starting to follow it back, only looking for A. Titania.

"I'm guessing that's the trunk line that snagged us", said Sarah. "Must have snapped like a rubber band."

I fully opened the camera aperture to grab any reflected light that this heartless void could offer. My eyes combed every pixel, like I was starving and looking for crumbs. I scrutinized the drifting trunk line meter by meter, eventually back to its anchor on the web that was grainy in the dim light. But there was no A. Titania. I felt tears begin to well up; I exhaled and closed my eyes tight. I rubbed them to appear fatigued to Sarah. I didn't want to her to know the heavy guilt that sank my soul. I let go of the articulator and let the camera drift.

"Hey!" she said.

Great, I thought, *now she knows and I have to deal with that, too.*

But then she continued, "What's over there?" I opened my eyes and looked at the monitor where Sarah pointed. In the distance, something was tumbling away from us and toward the web.

I centered the camera on the object and zoomed in. It was she! But I couldn't tell if she was alive. She was curled tight; I could make out the limbs clasped around the body. I tracked her trajectory back toward the web. Then she impacted the web and her limbs sprang open, she grabbed on tight, then scrambled away.

"Yes!" I shouted, punching my fist into the air.

Sarah turned from the monitor to look at me with some consternation. "Are you okay?" she asked.

"I have never felt better!" I beamed.

━━━━

The weeks that followed our return to base were filled with repairs to the sub and debriefings as missing pieces of the puzzle fell into place. The oxygen-methane explosion freed the *Nemo* and we were able to ascend because the heavy oxygen ballast had been jettisoned. Also, much welcomed, was the upgrade to *Nemo's* sonar that had been blind to the web.

Far more profound missing pieces remained. What ecosystem could support A. Titania? Did subsurface conduits connect the surface seas? Were there passages to even greater subsurface reservoirs? But these were idle musings compared to a question more unnerving than intriguing: Was Arachnida Titania the apex predator?

We set sail tomorrow, beneath an umber sky.

VENUSIAN
PARADISE

THE INVERSE OF guacamole crashed Mr. Foodster and sent a shockwave through Paradise. Simeon stared at the error message, fists clenched. He shouted across the living room, "Hey! What does 'System Trap 104' mean? I ordered inverse guacamole and got that message."

Twenty meters away, past the Monet, around the koi pond, and under the Chihuly chandelier, Chip and Elle were planted on the wraparound couch. They stayed focused on a house of cards being built on the mahogany coffee table. Floor-level picture windows revealed a panoramic view of Venusian cloud tops, above which floated Chip's lighter-than-air habitat, Paradise. Filtered sunlight slanted in from the windows high up the side of the balloon that was both their ceiling and their sky.

Elle carefully positioned a card. "It means you busted it with your stupid order." The card successfully placed, Chip exhaled. He leaned over to give Elle a peck on the cheek, but she had to meet him halfway as he was somewhat anchored by his girth. They looked with satisfaction at the second layer of the house that was now complete. Elle beamed and applauded herself.

By now, Simeon had sulked back to plop onto the couch. "Damn it… I wanted to try inverse guacamole with inverse chips."

Chip finally looked up. "Did you reboot it, or whatever?"

"It just did the spinning ball thing, so I turned it off."

Elle erupted, her tight mainspring always one tick away from cathartic unspooling. "You what?! That can bust it! How are we supposed to eat? Inverse guacamole. What an idiot." Unsatisfied with Simeon's lack of remorse, she barked, "Fix it! Go downstairs and… fix it!"

Chip was bemused. Simeon and Elle never failed to deliver as his personal Punch and Judy show. In a rare cameo, he added, "You break it, you buy it!"

Simeon didn't budge and deadpanned, "Ha ha." As a final incentive, Elle flung a small pillow at him. He dodged the pillow, which knocked over a framed picture on the end table and sent it skidding across the tile floor. But it wasn't just any picture. Simeon and Elle looked at each other, aghast, then slowly turned to see Chip's reaction. The humor drained from his face, his gray eyes turned cold, and he extended his hand. Simeon retrieved the picture, relieved that it appeared intact, and delicately handed it to Chip as if it was lifted from a Pharaoh's crypt.

Chip inspected the framed photograph for damage. Seven people stood for an informal portrait in front of an unremarkable office building. Chip was far to the left, at the edge of the frame, at perhaps half his current weight. Behind them was the company name, "ExWhy, Inc." The autographs alone would be valuable collectibles. The globe-spanning enterprise had made everyone in the picture vastly wealthy. They were the first seven employees, "The Magnificent Seven!" as the founder had written across the bottom. Chip was #7. There was no Elle or Simeon; they came much later, after the money, attracted like ants to a mountain of sugar.

As Chip studied the picture, memories of that day long ago flashed back. He recalled that he was almost not in the picture. As the startup's gofer, he was asked to take the picture. The caption would have been "The Magnificent Six!" had Chip not suggested to prop the camera on a post and use its timer. He would still have the wealth, but he wouldn't have been part of the band. He wouldn't have been magnificent like the others; he would have just been the gofer who took the picture.

The mood had turned somber, and Simeon made his way to the stairway, crestfallen. "If I'm not back in 24 hours, send down a search party."

Back at the couch, the photograph was returned to its place of honor. The house of cards project resumed.

From somewhere deep beneath the living room, giant propellers started to spin, but their soft hum was practically lost behind the bubbling of the koi pond. Their push was so gentle that the house of cards stood, as it always had. The fish were immune to the subtle rocking that shifted the water level back and forth. Like the rest of Paradise, the propellers were solar powered. They would occasionally spin up to keep Paradise in the northern hemisphere of the tidally locked planet, safely away from the South Polar Vortex. Except for these carefully timed pushes, Paradise was smoothly carried by ceaseless winds, 200 kilometers per hour strong here at 50 kilometers above the surface hellscape. It drifted as aimlessly as a swimming pool float, and her passengers were just as passive. Chip and Elle inhabited their card house and ignored the slowly swinging chandelier overhead.

Simeon turned around a corner from the living room and walked along a narrow hallway to the door. He swung it open to the much more distinct sound of propeller motors and the odors of machine oil and ozone that wafted up from Utility Deck 1. He felt for the light switch and held onto the handrail as he descended the steep, narrow steps. He hated to go down there.

At the bottom of the steps he paused to look down the narrow aisle that divided the floor. Somewhere back there was the Mr. Foodster synthesizing unit. On each side were racks of equipment and supply cabinets. Bright overhead spotlights dotted the path. The trek began as he walked by an empty storage locker, ducked to avoid a low pipe, and then past a cramped, filthy bathroom. He was careful not to brush against any of the grimy surfaces. In this lower level, suspended further from the balloon's center of gravity, the gentle rocking was more pronounced. There was even Utility Deck 2 beneath this one, which he imagined rocked even more. He explored there once when he first arrived, but never again. It had batteries and motors for the propellers and was terribly cramped and hot. If he thought about the rocking, he might get seasick. The overhead point lights cast strong shadows, which seemed to amplify the sense of motion. To take his mind off of this, he focused on the search for the garish "Mr. Foodster" logo. The propellers turned off, which was a relief and helped him to concentrate.

Although the trek took perhaps 30 minutes, it seemed like ages before Simeon found the Mr. Foodster unit near the end of the long aisle, crowded against three escape pods. A small window admitted a view of the cloud tops filtered by a grimy film. He unplugged the unit and waited for its row of lights to wink off. Then he plugged it back in and waited until the lights seemed finished with their imponderable startup sequence. He crossed his fingers, flipped the 'On' switch, and prayed for a successful boot-up. While Mr. Foodster whined and chirped, there was a swoosh of water from above. A toilet had flushed. *Probably Elle.* The water recycling system activated nearby, which compounded the din.

Mr. Foodster didn't cooperate. 'System Trap 104' persisted. "Dammit!"

Simeon trudged back to the stairs and then up into the wide-open elegance of the living room. He had to deliver the bad news, but it was heavenly to take a breath of fresh air in the daylight. It was the same breathable air that filled the entire balloon, buoyant in Venus' carbon dioxide atmosphere. Some lighter-than-air habitats were aviaries with songbirds that flitted about. But not

Paradise, with its Impressionist masterworks and other priceless art. The din from downstairs was replaced by a Mozart piano concerto that played softly; the chandelier caught sunlight that angled from above and scattered chromatic splashes.

Elle turned from the liquor cabinet where she had just refilled a tumbler with her favorite single malt scotch, now sipped from an unsteady hand. Chip looked up from the growing house of cards. "Well?"

"Looks like leftovers for a while."

Chip and Elle moaned in unison.

Simeon cast his eyes at the floor. "Sorry."

"He apologized!" shouted Elle, in mock amazement. "You heard it. He apologized." She began to slur her words. "Everything'll be fine now."

"Enough," commanded Chip. Elle clammed up. She managed to return to the couch. Simeon found a chair across the room.

Chip picked up a phone and placed a call. After a long wait, the threadbare network of satellites and relay blimps connected to an automated support system that floated in a depot thousands of kilometers away. Venusian habitation was the province of the intrepid super wealthy or scientists; communication was unreliable and product support was a rare and expensive luxury, but one that Chip could afford.

After a tiresome exchange with the automated system, the call ended and Chip announced the resolution. "They did the troubleshooting and, yeah, it's busted." Elle's protests had been pre-empted by his raised hand. "They will replace it, but it will take a few months." The hand stayed raised and Elle squirmed as she struggled to comply while unhinged by the scotch. "I have Platinum coverage, so..." he waited for the dramatic pause to build. Simeon and Elle were rapt. "They are sending over someone to work the kitchen! A *person* will cook our meals and clean our dishes until Mr. Foodster can be replaced! They'll be here in a couple days."

Elle and Simeon cheered.

The flurry of the excitement passed, and Paradise's residents returned to the house of cards, its third level almost complete.

Daniel tightened the seat belt around his duffel bag as Millie hollered from the cockpit over the screaming engines. "Buckle up, son. We got a long trip and we're burning fuel." He could only see the back of her head, curly salt-and-pepper hair, turning from side to side to monitor the instruments. Above the control panel was a posted small picture of an infant; a grandchild, he presumed.

"I'm moving as fast as I can!" The duffel bag secure, he slung the shoulder strap across his chest and buckled the waist belt. "OK! Let 'er rip!" He sat back and braced, a book clenched in his hands. He had the three-hour trip to read "Mr. Foodster Recipes for Dummies."

Millie gave a gravel-voiced, "Roger that," and reached up to grab two red latches on the flight deck overhead panel. The latches held the craft tightly against the belly of the vast Northern Depot blimp. With Daniel onboard, the docking exercise was complete. Now, it was time to deliver the passenger. With a swift yank, the latches released, and the ship dropped. Daniel's stomach floated, suddenly queasy. Millie vectored the thrust once the ship had fallen free, which shoved Daniel's stomach back into place. The jet swept away from the Northern Depot that floated above and blocked the view of the hazy sulfuric acid clouds.

The thrust pressed Daniel into his seat; his eyes felt squished into his head. Could the engines get any louder? Apparently, they could. The ship banked and Daniel fought the acceleration to turn his head and get a clear view of the blimp that filled half the sky at this distance, its silver skin catching the sunset as the winds carried it toward the twilight. Several other craft were attached to the blimp or maneuvering through their vertical approaches and flight.

The craft found its vector and leveled off as the engines diminished to a sustainable roar. They were bound for Paradise, thousands of kilometers into the sunlit side of Venus. It meant fighting the prevailing wind, so Millie maneuvered to a higher altitude. "We'll burn a lot of fuel heading out, but it'll be a cakewalk coming back... I may even end up with a quarter tank."

Daniel noticed that he was breathing easy again. Riding these small jet transports was like being tethered to a roller coaster. Now that the flight had steadied, he decided to read the book. As a Foodster Inc. engineer, he had good knowledge of the system components and troubleshooting. But, for this case, those skills were not required. A Platinum class customer needed a cook and, as of today, Daniel's schedule had the most availability, so his number came up. That was a reality of interplanetary duty. It was time to become a cook.

On Paradise, the central timer clocked off another day. Hours ago, the array of window shades had silently descended to shut out the oppressive sun. Warm mood lighting softly glowed. Simeon had shoveled together and heated a meal of leftovers, which meant another thankless trip downstairs.

Now the central timer muted the tranquil background music, dimmed the living room lights, and turned on the bedroom lights. The habitat was cooled to invite cozy repose. Although there were three bedrooms, rarely were they all used in a night. Chip generally preferred company, which often included Elle but sometimes Simeon; sometimes both. Tonight, however, Simeon spent a gloomy night alone, in the dog house.

Millie tweaked the trajectory to avoid turbulence and charted a course via a clear stratospheric layer between opaque yellow cloud strata above and below. The sun was higher and saturated the view with harsh brilliance.

Daniel fought boredom as he read recipes and planned how to use the crippled Mr. Foodster to create the dishes. He had progressed to "D" and "Danish Ham." Thoughts wandered to concerns about the customer. Platinum customers could be demanding and the fact that this one had their own private habitat didn't bode well. He went back to recipes to keep from worrying.

After several hours, Millie spoke up, matter-of-fact: "There's the target." Daniel figured she was former military.

A bright ellipsoid floated far ahead in the same clear stratum. While certainly much smaller than the Northern Depot, it was easily the largest private habitat he had ever seen or heard of. As they drew close enough to see detail, no other craft was docked to it. The living space looked perhaps a thousand square meters, several stories high, built into the enclosed balloon. Daniel was spellbound and wondered how many people lived there.

The jet dipped as they approached the underside of the habitat structure. Millie muttered to herself as she hunted for the docking port. Then red concentric circles, dotted with blinking lights, came into view. "There it is! Sit tight, son. We're going to dock soon."

Daniel cinched the belts, which were already tight.

Millie rotated the engines into a vertical holding attitude under the docking ring. The jet rocked and then steadied. She followed protocol to announce, "Paradise. JSX 1200. Preparing to dock." After a moment of silence, she repeated the announcement. No reply.

Daniel gazed up to search for some sign of life, though unsure what to expect. "I wonder what time it is here."

"Whatever time they want." Then she improvised a new announcement: "Cock-a-doodle do! Ready or not, here we come!" Alas, the Paradise intercoms were shut off while the passengers slept. Millie turned to Daniel and added, "Let's see if they left a key under the mat." The jet rose and snagged the docking ring. The overhead latches engaged. Millie gave a thumbs up and shut down the engines.

The silence and stillness were pure bliss, though Daniel's body still felt phantom vibration. Millie opened the docking hatch and the heavy door swung down.

Daniel unbuckled, eager to move again and even more eager to meet his new clients after the faulty unit was stowed. He clambered up the ladder and onto Utility Deck 2. A quick check showed that he needed to press on, so he did; Millie followed.

On Deck 1, he pitched the duffel bag into the storage locker, grimaced at the site of the unclean bathroom, and soon found the Mr. Foodster unit. He knew this drill well and promptly decoupled the faulty component. With Millie's help, they carried it back down to the jet, where it was stowed.

"Thanks for the ride, Millie. You might as well take off... I'll poke round." She gave a friendly salute and disappeared down the hatch. Moments later, back on Deck 1, Daniel felt a shudder through the floor and heard the whine of jet engines as Millie departed.

He looked himself over. The lengthy flight had left his clothes badly wrinkled and now they were smudged with grime. He wanted to clean and change but had no living quarters yet.

Upstairs, the central timer clocked the start of a new day. The blinds rose and a spirited flute solo floated through the living room. Elle shuffled out of Chip's bedroom and over to the coffee machine which, mercifully, was not part of Mr. Foodster. By the time her café latte was prepared, she felt a tap on the shoulder. Chip had waddled out. "Gimme. Please." With a pout, Elle surrendered her coffee and prepared another. She went back to the couch where Chip had settled, joined by a yawning Simeon. The three sat in their robes and bedclothes.

Invariably, attention turned to the house of cards. But then, from across the room, someone cleared their throat.

Elle screamed at the sight of Daniel standing next to koi pond, cookbook in hand. Simeon grabbed a candlestick and feigned an offensive posture. Chip noticed the cookbook. "You must be from Mr. Foodster. I am Chip and these are my friends, Elle and Simeon." Then, with a dramatic flourish, "Welcome to Paradise, my humble home."

Daniel absorbed the reception and composed himself. "Yes, thank you. I am Daniel Kehoe; you can call me Dan." He wished he had rehearsed an introduction. After a self-conscious cough, he defaulted to the usual professional verbiage. "I have a graduate degree in mechanical engineering, two food synthesis patents, and over five years of experience designing and maintaining Mr. Foodster synthesizers. It will be my pleasure to help with your food service until you have a fully functioning Mr. Foodster."

"Oh, the cook!" cheered Elle, with spirited clapping. "Perfect timing! Run downstairs and whip up breakfast!"

Simeon added, "Can you make inverse guacamole?! And inverse chips?!" That triggered an automatic, "Shut up!" from Elle, all of which amused Chip.

Daniel knew his place and replied, respectfully, "Sorry, but I can't prepare inverse foods. That requires the machine learning unit, which has been removed." Simeon groaned. Daniel held up the cookbook, "I can try anything in this. But I'd like to move in first." He looked around the living room. "Which bedroom is mine?"

Chip laughed so hard that he snorted, which triggered an Elle and Simeon giggle fit. Chip recovered first and wiped away tears. "You'll stay downstairs. We haven't room up here." He turned to Elle and Simeon. "Please show our cook to the downstairs accommodations." Elle and Simeon suddenly acted effete and rose to comply.

Daniel scanned the cavernous and luxurious living space. *They can't be serious.*

"Come along!" chirped Elle, a spring in her step. With a self-satisfied smile, Simeon graciously gestured toward the door. "I know the way," came Daniel's dry reply.

The trio descended, Elle first, feeling her way in the dark until Daniel flipped on the light. They gathered at the bottom of the stairs where Simeon used the same smug gesture to indicate the storage locker. "Please make yourself at home. You can move those boxes somewhere else; maybe downstairs. We will bring down some bedding." Daniel felt like a slave being shown his quarters, which, perhaps, was uncomfortably close to the truth. He struggled to fight the self-defeating attitude. *No point digging myself into a hole.... especially if I already live in one.*

Elle stepped to the bathroom entrance, careful to duck under the pipe. "And here is your lavatory." Daniel counted his breaths to stay composed. She continued, with an air of authority that papered over an utter lack of credibility. "You will, of course, wash your hands before preparing a meal. We'll take breakfast in the sun room. Just give a holler if you get lost!" Elle and Simeon savored the rare joy of the unaccomplished dishing out humiliation. Then they practically pranced up the stairs.

Daniel regrouped; he decided to score points and recover his standing with a successful first meal. A check of the inventory found the Mr. Foodster supply cabinets well stocked and in good order, a huge relief. He washed and prepared a safe recipe: A ham and eggs breakfast with orange juice and a side of buttered toast. The meal preparation was smooth. *So far, so good.*

He stacked the serving dishes on a tray and proceeded down the aisle. The propellers started and the floor began to sway. He stopped to steady the tray with its tower of dishes. *What's next?* He found his sea legs and gingerly balanced the tray. As he neared the stairway, the door opened and, over Simeon's giggles, a payload of sheets and blankets was heaved down and landed on the floor in front of him, raising a plume of dust. A pillow followed and the giggles only ended when the door slammed shut.

"Paradise" had already begun to wear thin but there was no choice except to push ahead. Daniel sighed and deftly navigated over and around the rudely delivered linens. After a careful turn, he started up the steep stairs; the dishes rattled with each step. The door handle opened with a press of his elbow on a lever, and he emerged into the first world ambiance that was inhabited by troglodytes.

After a quick scan, he spied them sitting in the "sun room," which was a sun-bathed dining nook with the table placed against a picture window. Simeon waved unnecessarily. Daniel pasted on a smile as he approached. They had changed into their day clothes and preened for the occasion to be waited upon. He served the meal; his wrinkled and smudged clothes scarcely masked simmering disgust.

Simeon took a sip of orange juice and grimaced. "Ewww... pulp!" Then, as though preparing for a charge at Gallipoli, he bravely drank the juice. With a cough, he added, "No pulp next time, Daniel."

Elle tapped an empty espresso cup with a spoon and looked up with a condescending smile.

Chip enjoyed the show as he wolfed down the meal.

Daniel was torn. His job was to provision meals, not act as butler. But here he was, with few options. If they could appreciate his cooking and if they just got to know him, then who knew? Maybe, just maybe, he could stay upstairs instead of in the pit. On the other hand, first impressions lasted. If he prepared this espresso, then he'd become the butler.

After a moment's deliberation, he stepped to the espresso machine and prepared Elle's drink. It was worth the gamble.

Daniel had last eaten at the Northern Depot and was famished. Yet they consumed the breakfast with such gusto that he saw no reason to leave only to return to clean up. He scrambled to pick up the dishes. After a brisk walk, he descended to his residence, which had all of the charm and comfort of a World War Two submarine. But, for now, it was refuge.

He prepared and ate a meal and then proceeded to move in, to make the hole into a home. He cleared and swept out the storage locker, then spread out the bedding. Clothes were hung from various brackets meant to secure tools. The bathroom was conquered next. To mark that success, he sat on the bedding and opened the duffel bag to dig out a sketch pad and a box of colored pencils.

The propellers spun up.

Daniel flipped to a work in progress, the drawing of a bouquet. As he reflected on the day's indignities, he decided to draw a fallen petal. He returned to the rest of the flowers, but before he could add blush to the lilacs, he was asleep, lulled by the gentle rocking of the propellers.

Simeon's voice burst through the intercom. "Ding ding! Hey Chip, we need a real bell. Daniel, we are ready for lunch!" Laughter followed, after which Elle added, "He said we can call him *Dan*." Laughter. "But that sounds rather... familiar. *Daniel*, we'll dine at the couch. Cold cuts are fine... but no pulp!" More mirth.

Daniel grasped that this was, indeed, reality to which he awoke. Memories of breakfast welled up like an overflowing toilet. He turned over and ached from the thin bedding.

Before responding to the onerous demand, Daniel paused to add another fallen petal to the drawing.

Simeon shouted again, "Hey Daniel! Can you hear us?"

Daniel stood, straightened, and stepped into the aisle to the intercom. "I hear you. I will bring up cold cuts."

"Very good, Daniel!" chirped Elle, followed by the customary laughter.

Over time, the drawings accumulated layers of fallen petals. Daniel was forced to concede that it was simply too delicious for Elle and Simeon to possess a downstairs minion. But Chip stayed above the fray; was he bored by the denigration? Or maybe, just maybe, did Chip have second thoughts about his treatment?

The shipment with the replacement Mr. Foodster unit was still months from Venus. But only two weeks into the assignment, his fantasies alternated between drugging their food with sedatives and bailing in an escape pod. He knew those musings were just to preserve his strained sanity. His drawings were an escape, but he knew that he would have to draw many more fallen petals.

Daniel took small solace in a couple of concessions, although they were granted with an air of noblesse oblige by Elle and Simeon: He was no longer on coffee duty. Also, he was invited to join them occasionally for movies, but he had to bring the popcorn and drinks.

<hr>

Daniel gazed out the window adjacent to the defunct Mr. Foodster as he prepared the evening's dinner. Paradise still floated in brilliant sunlight, but the slender burnt orange shadow of twilight tinged the distant horizon ahead. Serenity and solitude brought relief from the abuse. The calm evoked earlier naive hopes to live upstairs, but now he shook his head at the juxtaposition. In a few weeks the replacement Mr. Foodster should arrive; he could persevere, like a rodent amidst the dinosaurs.

Dishes and ingredients were arranged across the tops of the escape pods, which made a convenient staging area. He assembled the portions and then followed the well-established serving routine. He carried the tray up the stairs and to the dinner dining area where they sat. Elle and Simeon bickered as always, as Chip enjoyed.

In the midst of serving, the routine was shattered by a nerve-jarring claxon from the communication console across the room. Daniel almost dropped the tray when Elle's mainspring popped and she shrieked. The message scrolled across the large screen as it was spoken:

"This is an emergency alert from the Space Weather Prediction Center. A Critical Severity coronal mass ejection has been observed. There is a high probability of direct impact within eight hours after which lethal plasma intensity is expected for up to 20 hours. For the lethal period, anyone currently in the sun-facing hemisphere must either retreat to a Category A shielded environment or evacuate the hemisphere. Relocation of phone repeaters will disable phone service."

The message repeated, over animation of the solar wind pelting the sun-facing side of Venus. It showed a habitat like Paradise, coated with photovoltaics and embedded with electronics, spark like a Van de Graaf generator. Chip's phone displayed a status message, "Service unavailable."

The room fell silent. Daniel had stepped to the window to consider the distance to twilight and safety.

Chip spoke first, as he reached to hold Elle's and Simeon's hands. "We'll be fine. The escape pods are Category A." They squeezed hands and sighed with relief. Simeon sobbed and was consoled by Chip and Elle. "We'll be fine," repeated Chip with a reassuring smile as he patted Simeon's hand.

The words landed on Daniel like a load of bricks. They must know there were only three pods, but even these people couldn't be so cold. "Excuse me, but don't these giant habitats have more than three pods?"

Chip relied, "Indeed," which thrilled Daniel, until Chip continued, "It had four; alas, I had one removed to make room for Mr. Foodster."

Daniel felt empty, invisible, as immaterial as a shadow. How many times had he fantasized jumping into a pod and bailing? A balloon would inflate to keep the pod aloft, a transponder would send the distress signal, and he'd be rescued from this asylum. Why not do that now? Let them fend for themselves; draw straws, or fight it out?

As though he had read Daniel's mind, Chip added, "Don't get any ideas, my friend."

"What am I supposed to do!?"

Simeon finished wiping his tear-reddened eyes. "Mind the fort."

The callous remark was the last straw. Daniel lunged at Simeon and grabbed a chair to fling at him. Elle screamed and Chip commanded him to stop, but all of the power was Daniel's. Simeon scrambled to escape but stumbled over a serving table and fell hard against the mahogany table. The house of cards collapsed. He winced and crawled on the floor over scattered dishes and food. Daniel charged, then stood astride him, and raised the chair to crush Simeon's skull. Nothing else mattered. He would put this worm out of its misery and then escape in a pod to take his chances. But the invertebrate writhed as he pleaded; he cried apologies, hands clasped to beg for mercy. Daniel's chest heaved. Elle and Chip watched, more unwilling than unable to help their friend. Daniel's heart slowed its primeval beat. His breathing calmed and he placed the chair on the floor next to Simeon, who backed away, clothes smeared with the food he'd crawled through.

Daniel sat on the chair, put his face in his hands, and sobbed.

Chip was struck by the psychic shrapnel. He was silent and surveyed the scene of the paroxysm. He looked past Simeon to fix his gaze on Daniel. Thoughts returned to the ExWhy photograph and the marginalized gofer. *What kind of Paradise have I created?*

Daniel heard the creak of Chip's chair as the obese man rose and shuffled toward him. He felt Chip's warm hand on his shoulder, a squeeze, and then words flowed like brandy served to a man in agony. "It is a lot to ask. You will be doing me a great favor." With a solid pat on his back, Chip added, "Look up… Look around."

Daniel wiped his eyes on his sleeve and sniffed as he looked at the familiar scene. "What? Look at what?"

"Pick anything you want. It's yours."

Daniel looked up at Chip, tears streaming, "I want to live!"

"You will be taking a chance for the rest of us. We have no other choice."

Daniel struggled with yet another layer of Paradise insanity, bewildered by his fate and what amounted to a once-in-a-lifetime opportunity. Still, despite the cognitive and emotional whirlwind, he was confident of the answer. He pointed to a Monet oil painting. It was a bouquet of sunflowers, with no fallen petals, that would be the centerpiece of any major art museum. "That."

From behind him, Daniel heard Elle say under her breath, "No!"

Chip extended his hand to shake. "Done; I promise." Daniel lifted his hand to reciprocate; Chip grabbed it and sealed the deal with a firm handshake.

Elle repeated whispered admonishments. Chip turned to her, "Hush!" She pursed her lips.

Like magic, the painting lifted Daniel's mind away from the pending hazard, at least for now. He seized the moment. "Let's get this over with. They said the plasma forecast is just an estimate. We may not have much time before it hits, so let's go down and get ready." Simeon limped to his room for a quick change of clothes.

They followed Daniel down the stairs. Chip studied each stair step and gripped both handrails. "I was down here once several years ago, when I arrived." At the bottom of the stairs, the group turned and walked past the storage locker. Chip noticed the bedding and turned to Daniel. "Your bedroom?" Daniel nodded.

Chip poked his head inside and saw the colored pencil sketches of bouquets stuck to the wall. Daniel's tenderly wrought splashes of color contrasted with the spartan and utilitarian setting. The sight moved Chip, always fortified, king of his castle, to be stabbed by an icy pang of guilt. He stood there, astonished by the claustrophobic room, and searched for words. "Um… your new painting will fit right in." Daniel had nothing to say.

The journey to the pods continued; Chip remained preoccupied by the upstairs scene and now this.

They reached the end where the remains of dinner preparation covered the pods. Elle and Simeon were uncommonly silent, cowed. Without being asked, they pitched in to clear off the dishes and utensils. The escape pods were cylinders, about one-and-a-half meters in diameter and three meters tall, though much of the height was below the floor. A ladder built into the outside permitted access through a hatch on top.

Simeon unlatched and opened a pod, then proceeded to climb up and in. "No time like the present!" The padded seat inside was laced with safety belts and Simeon managed to secure himself. He looked up at the three faces peering down. Controls to activate air filtration and other life support were straightforward and clearly labelled. With a sunny smile, he gave two thumbs up.

A bright red plunger had a yellow "EJECT" on the handle. Chip pointed to it, "Don't pull that." The comment triggered Elle and Simeon to laugh, until they noticed that Chip was stone-faced. He turned to Daniel, whose sober expression showed that he was far removed from any levity. With a conciliatory expression, Chip added, "We'll stay inside until the coast is clear. Our friend here will let us know when it's time to come out... Knock three times." Daniel nodded.

"But he might be..." started Elle, avoiding eye contact with the others.

Chip rebuked her. "You can be quite cruel, young lady."

Simeon had been distracted by his pod's interior. "There is a data feed in here... And it just posted an update. Let's see.... They have a better mapping of the wavefront and... reading... reading... gosh... they say the first lethal plasma may hit *within three hours*." Chip acknowledged the news as he maintained a severe expression. Simeon decided that it was time to reach up and close the hatch.

Elle was next. "Well... better safe than sorry." Lithe and motivated, she practically poured into the second pod. After a more subdued thumbs up, she reached to close the hatch.

Finally, it was time for Chip. Daniel knew this could be a tight fit. Chip opened the hatch and smiled as he turned to Daniel. "Do you have some butter to grease this thing?" Then he leaned heavily on Daniel and took careful steps up the side ladder; he puffed from the modest exertion. Chip sat on the top of the pod, legs hanging over the side ladder, and caught his breath. Then he pivoted to sit on the edge of the hatch and dangle his legs into the pod. He twisted to look back at Daniel and chuckled. "Like two pounds of baloney going into a one-pound bag." Daniel grinned, though it seemed like the joke had more than a grain of truth.

Chip lifted his body with his arms to let his weight pull him into the pod. But it only compressed the spreading girth to turn him into an obese cork. He raised his arms and stayed stuck. He waved them around and burst into peals of laughter at the ludicrous situation; tears streamed down his beet red face. At first, Daniel was still unable to laugh but this was like a scene from a Laurel and Hardy movie. He finally loosened and joined the laughter, a welcome wash of relief.

Chip managed to extricate himself and swung around to hang his legs over the side ladder again. "Looks like I'm not going anywhere." He put his arms out for Daniel to help him down, which he did. Chip took a towel and wiped the tears and sweat from his face as he caught his breath. Then, with a grandiose sweep of his arm, he gestured to the ladder, "After you, sir."

The offer stunned Daniel. Every day since he arrived, he was treated as second-class, even practically expendable. It made the offer tantalizing and almost irresistible. But, tempting as it was, he couldn't fathom sharing the same sanctuary as Elle and Simeon, while Chip was sacrificed. Daniel raised his hands and took a step back from the pod. "No, there's still time… there has to be a better way."

Chip shook his head and turned to look out the window. "I don't see how." The twilight arc was still slender and remote. "The announcement said to move out of the sun-facing side. Paradise is drifting toward the twilight but will never get there in time."

Daniel paced back and forth in the narrow space in front of the pods, head bowed and eyes closed in thought.

The propellers spun up. The unaccustomed wide rocking on this deck caught Chip off-guard and he steadied himself. Then his face lit with inspiration: "The propellers!" He grabbed Daniel and looked him in the eyes. "Maybe we could get there fast enough with the help of the propellers."

"Chip, can you fly this thing!?"

"Oh, good heavens, no. I don't even know how to steer it." He searched for the answer in Daniel's eyes. "Could you figure it out? I mean, you are an engineer…." The words trailed off.

Daniel was jolted by the absurdity. "Me?"

Chip was undeterred. "Then maybe we can put our heads together." He started the long walk to the stairs, as the rocking made him chafe on the sides of aisle.

Daniel followed. The exchange raised a question that nagged him since his arrival, but it hadn't been appropriate to ask. Surely, someone who could purchase a lavish mansion that floats over Venus has achieved something extraordinarily valuable. Surely, they have a profound talent.

Daniel decided that, in light of the circumstance, there was no need for unearned deference. "Excuse me, but how exactly did you make your fortune?"

Chip assumed a sage countenance and pondered the question as they walked. "Ah, the question everyone wants to ask me... but few are bold enough." He drew a deep breath. "You know, for others, it's obvious. Like you, they may have patents, or perhaps they've authored a shelf full of books. But look around and you will only see that I surrounded myself with possessions that comfort me, inspire me, or..." with a backwards nod toward the occupied pods "... amuse me." Several silent steps followed. "But... I have created nothing."

It felt tragic, as though he had confessed to an unfulfilled life.

Chip continued, "Have you heard of a company named 'ExWhy'?"

"Of course! Everyone has. I probably use ExWhy every day back on Earth."

"I was employee #7. Hired way before they went public, got a bunch of stock options, and voila!"

"Wow! What was your role? It must have been pretty important to be hired so early in the company's life."

"Important? How about I was on the same college intramural volleyball team as the founder? They needed someone to work for free. It was summer vacation; I had nothing better to do. I was a starving Anthropology undergrad, so why not? I started as an office manager, really just a glorified gofer. Then I became a project manager, that is, I learned how to become a project manager." He chuckled. "That's it. No secret sauce, no patent, no mastery of anything. When ExWhy grew, well, my responsibilities grew with it. You know, find a need and fill it. I ended up having a great time, aside from the money. It was a great team." He sighed. "It's like a successful Broadway play that had its run; after the last curtain call, the actors move on and the magic is just a memory. But, God, I miss it."

As they passed his storage locker bedroom, Daniel tried to soak up the incongruity of it all but it was too much to digest. There was important work to do, truly important, not in the form of lucky timing as with Chip's volleyball team. There was a real problem to solve: A matter of life and death.

At the base of the stairs was one flight up to the residence and another down to Deck 2. Chip turned to Daniel. "Well? Up or down?" Daniel shrugged, then pointed down.

Daniel opened the door to the loud whine of the motors and flipped on a light switch. They stepped down the stairs, Daniel first, to assist in case Chip should stumble. In addition to the noise, the room was uncomfortably warm. Chip began to sweat. Giant batteries and massive electric motors stretched for perhaps fifty meters. Suddenly there was a sequence of clicks from somewhere across the room. The routine push had ended, and the motors stopped.

The silence allowed Chip to offer his tidbits of information. "From what I understand, the purpose of all of this is to keep Paradise from drifting into the southern hemisphere. There is something dangerous down there... a vortex."

Daniel knew of the feature. "The South Polar Vortex."

Chip nodded. "Right." Sweat began to soak through his shirt. "And if a habitat like this gets caught in the vortex, well, it just swirls around and around." He whirled his finger. "Can't get out. The winds are pretty fierce. They would just tear it apart and then... next stop, the hellscape."

Daniel scratched his head, lost in thought. "There's no GPS or magnetic field. Cannot see stars. I wonder how it keeps track of location? I wonder how it can be steered? I'm going on a walkabout. Give a shout if you find something." He marched off to reconnoiter.

Chip looked around the room, which was as inscrutable to him as an alien spaceship. He hollered to Daniel, who had made it almost half way to the far end. "Dan! Where do the motors and batteries meet? Maybe the brain is there!"

Daniel paused for an instant to savor that one word. *Dan.* "All of these cabinets definitely hold the batteries and…" he continued at a brisk pace, "… and here is where the motors start."

Chip had started to make his way and fixed his gaze on what, from this distance, looked like a chair in front of some sort of console. He waved his arm, pointing at the console. "Over there!" Chip charged ahead but grew winded and had to slow down. Daniel arrived at the console first and shouted back, "I think you found it!"

A few minutes later, Chip arrived and Daniel yielded the seat which Chip flopped into, and breathed a sigh of relief. He used his sleeve to mop off his brow. But then something caught his eye, the edge of a flat object on top of the console. He was promptly back on his feet to study it. It was a raised square, perhaps five by five centimeters, in which was inscribed a circle, perhaps four centimeters in diameter. Embossed in the circle was stylized script, "Pulsar Inertials"; the edge of the circle was marked like a protractor.

Daniel looked at the square. "I noticed that, but thought it was just a logo."

Chip rubbed his chin. "I own stock in that company. Lemme think… Pulsar Inertials…" A detail caught his eye. The square was held in placed by a screw in each corner, but a fifth, larger, screw had a different purpose. It was tucked next to the circle. "They have tech for spacecraft navigation. That's pretty much all I know; didn't expect to see them here." He looked around the deck. "Is Paradise a spacecraft? Well, anyway…"

Daniel touched the fifth screw, which was slightly raised. "That's a set screw."

Chip's face brightened. "Yes! To loosen the circle! Like positioning a sundial!" That started a scramble to find the key. Drawers were opened and Chip soon found it. He placed it in the set screw but then froze. He and Daniel stared at each other. "Dan, let's each think about which way to turn the disk. Then, we'll see if we get the same answer."

Daniel agreed. They each fell deep into thought, as hands moved to follow imaginary vector geometries. Daniel finished a minute later. "Ready."

Chip stayed lost in thought, but then looked up. "OK. I'll go first. It's positioned to keep us from drifting south, so that means it wants to go north when it's turned on. So... I think we want to rotate it 90-degrees clockwise to aim for the twilight."

Daniel smiled. "Yep, that's what I figured, too."

Chip loosened the screw and gave the disk a small budge. The motors roared to life. He looked at Daniel, who laughed and gave a thumbs up. Over the motor noise, Daniel shouted, "Keep going!" Chip advanced the disk and the gargantuan vessel pivoted. The motors whined even louder to make up for the perceived gap in the ship's orientation. They both had to shift their weight and adjust footing to counter the change in inertia. Daniel still laughed, but now it was because he pondered what Elle and Simeon must be thinking. It was the purest joy he'd felt in a long time.

Chip pointed up and they made their way to the stairs. They climbed to Deck 1, closed the door, and the deafening sound was muted. Daniel turned to Chip and gestured toward the pods. "Should we tell them?"

Chip chuckled. "Naw! Let's go up and look out the forward window." They made their way upstairs.

Paradise's abrupt turn had left the residence in a jumble. Furniture had slid or rolled; the living room had all of the feng shui of the scattered house of cards. Chip paused to marvel at the fantastic circular arc swept by the chandelier. A koi fish flopped on the tile and Daniel raced over, careful not to slip on the water that had sloshed out of the pond. The fish was reunited with its friends in the shallower water.

Daniel found Chip in the master suite; its picture window faced forward. Chip stood before the window, which perfectly framed the umber arc of twilight. "We did it." They stood side by side.

Their gazes fixed on the arc. They knew it had to widen enough to engulf Paradise in darkness before the plasma hit.

As they watched, the arc slightly expanded but remained stubbornly narrow.

Daniel was first to say the obvious, as he shook his head. "It may not have been enough." He glanced at his timepiece. "We've been looking for 20 minutes but we seem to be hanging here. The twilight looks almost the same as when I walked in here."

Chip nodded. "I know, but I want to believe." He tightened his fists, as though hope might otherwise slip away.

From the living room, the console blared another alarm. They walked to the door to hear the announcement.

"This is an emergency alert from the Space Weather Prediction Center. The plasma wavefront is expected to impact within two hours with lethal intensity. Anyone in the sun-facing hemisphere must proceed to a Category A shelter…"

The message continued, but they didn't listen.

Daniel turned back to glance at the twilight.

Chip smiled, as tears started to stream. "Let me guess… no change."

Daniel put his arm on his shoulder.

Chip wiped tears to take a wistful look at Paradise. "We were quite a team, Dan."

Daniel struggled to maintain focus, to scour for another possibility. Then a thought struck. "Don't give up yet."

Daniel ran out of the suite and headed for the stairs, rushed down to Deck 1, and raced to the pods. He pounded simultaneously on both occupied pods. They opened; Elle and Simeon peaked out like timid gophers. Daniel spoke as he caught his breath. "Listen! I don't have time to explain, but Chip cannot fit into his pod and we… the three of us… we each need to eject to increase the odds that one of us will be found." Their puzzled expressions showed he wasn't getting through. He rolled his eyes, exasperated. "I have spent a lot of time down here… and I have studied these pods… *a lot*. Don't ask why." They were startled, but Daniel pressed on. "When a pod ejects, a powerful rescue beacon activates and a balloon inflates to keep it aloft. One of us is bound to be found, then we can tell them to come back and get Chip."

Simeon spoke first. "Doesn't Paradise have a beacon thing?"

Daniel's fury with Simeon flared up again. "I don't know. And I am pretty sure that Chip doesn't know either. Do you want to climb out to look for it?" There was no reply. "I didn't think so. *See how I know that about you?* Look, regardless, it's simple: We are running out of time and the more of us out there, the better the odds someone will be picked up, then Chip and the rest of us can be rescued. *Don't worry, you'll be safe.* These have two weeks of life support. Someone will snag you."

The gophers silently retreated into their holes; the lids latched shut.

Daniel put them out of his mind, as best as he could, and concentrated on the next moves. He climbed into Chip's pod, secured the hatch, sat, and tightened himself in the web of safety belts. Now safe in the Category A pod, the "EJECT" plunger gave him brief pause. But his friend depended upon him.

He closed his eyes, gritted his teeth, and pulled the plunger. There was a sudden sideways shove and a scaping sound, then the instant nausea like when he dropped from of the Northern Depot.

Elle and Simeon felt the sudden shift. But after a quick validation of their pods' integrity, they settled back to their comfort and security. In the master suite, Chip had returned to the window and was shocked to see a large flashing red balloon drift from below. It pitched and rotated in the turbulence; the attached small escape pod briefly swung into view. "Dan... what have you done?"

In the escape pod, Daniel had a white-knuckle grip on the straps as the pod tumbled. It reminded him of the idiotic dare he took in college to climb into a clothes dryer. Hopefully, this was more sane. The status panel showed all green, including "Transponder: Full Power." Eventually, the bobbing and twisting dampened and the pod gently swayed beneath the balloon.

He felt like bait; was there a hungry fish nearby?

In the hours before the plasma wave hit, the *All Hands* call was put out to pilots to conduct search and rescue missions. Millie had ventured from safety and into the sunlight to sweep for anyone who may need assistance. A service jet like hers did not have Category A shielding, so it was essential to budget time to return before the plasma wave hit.

Daniel had drifted for almost an hour and the pod's transponder continued to blast its rescue signal. Like a cork bobbing in the ocean, he didn't know where he was or where he was going. If it wasn't a bid to save Chip's life, he could have been lulled to sleep. Then, against the almost perfect silence started a tiny shrill sound, like a mosquito. He looked at the instruments for a possible source, but the sound grew louder until it was obvious that it was from the outside.

The shrill rose to a sustained climax and the pod rocked as heavy metal pieces clanked. The pod violently lurched to the side and, as he lay on his back, still strapped into his seat, the hatch opened. He looked up to see a familiar face. "Well, look what I caught!" cheered Millie. "Come on aboard."

In a blur of hand waving, the straps were released and then Daniel pulled himself into Millie's jet. As he clambered in to the same seat he had occupied a few months ago, he asked, "Any other beacons?"

She reviewed the telemetry. "Nope. This picks up any beacon within a thousand klicks. Should there be?"

"I thought there might be a couple more, but I guess they stayed behind. Remember that mansion you took me to?"

Millie rechecked fuel supply and the latest plasma update. "Yep… We need to make another stop? There isn't much time."

"I'm afraid so."

"Hold on." She closed the pod hatch and punched a large red button. There was a whoosh and the jet pitched to the left. "Say bye bye to your pod. Don't want the weight."

"I ejected from the mansion over an hour ago but I wouldn't know how to find it."

She was lost in a frenzy of keystrokes. "OK, now we wait. I sent a broadcast trigger that should activate any rescue beacons out there.

I don't normally do that because we get a lot of false positives; you know, not everyone needs to be rescued, they are already in a shelter or they are nuts. But this sector is like a ghost town. Everyone cleared out and… Hold on. What have we here?" A scan showed a blinking dot. "Bingo! Buckle up!"

Daniel crossed fingers on both hands. "How long until the plasma hits?"

"It's complicated. Just sit tight." The engines rotated to horizontal and roared to full thrust.

The headwinds jostled the jet from side-to-side and Millie struggled to keep the jet on its trajectory. "No time to climb to clearer atmosphere. Barf bag is under the seat."

Daniel wished she hadn't said that; he dug his fingers into the armrests.

A red banner message flashed on the main console. "Plasma impact: 40 minutes." He looked out the window and expected to see something different, but it was the brilliant sun, now ochre-colored and low in the sky. He realized that the plasma was bound to hit Paradise.

After 10 minutes, Millie gave the announcement he hoped for. "There's the target." Paradise floated ahead. He loved Millie.

She continued. "I should've asked… how many are we picking up? We can carry four passengers; after that, everyone's luggage."

Daniel considered the irony of these accommodations compared to Paradise. "Just three more."

The jet swooped under Deck 2, hovered to line up with the docking ring, and then rose to engage. Millie shut off the engines; by the time she told Daniel to hurry, he had unbuckled and climbed to the hatch which had just opened. He flew up the ladder and the two flights of stairs to the living room.

"Chip! Chip! I'm back! There's a jet waiting! Let's go!" Across the chaos of the living room, Daniel saw Chip seated in front of the Monet. Chip stirred. Had he been asleep? Daniel rushed to him. On the floor was an empty wine bottle.

Chip looked up and his head wobbled. "I thought you left me. You… *bastard.*"

Daniel tugged to try and pull him out of the chair. "Yep, I'm a bastard. Now come on. I have a jet. We still have time and there is room for all of us."

Chip began to rouse. He grabbed the bottle, pointed at the label, and sighed sweetly, "Merlot." Then he pointed at the painting. "Monet. Both French. I wanted France to be in my last thoughts." His words slurred. "It's interesting… to consider what… one's last thoughts should be."

"Yeah, interesting." Daniel grabbed his arm. "Let's talk about it on the jet."

The facts finally clicked. "A jet!? You *son of a bitch!*" Daniel felt promoted and Chip stood to give him an alcohol imbued bear hug. He widened bloodshot eyes to clear his head. "OK… OK… I need to grab a couple of things. I'll be right behind you." Then, with an exasperated sigh, he pointed down. "I guess you might as well get the others."

Daniel imagined Millie's patience burning like a fuse. "Fine… But get down to the port on Deck 2. You know where?"

"Yes! Jesus! I am not that drunk!"

"Right." Daniel raced down to the pods. As he ran down the aisle, he noticed that some cabinets were open. The pods were already well stocked; had they come out to rummage for other food? He was surprised that he could be surprised by them.

He pounded on the pods like a madman. Both hatches opened and they peaked out, gopher-like again.

A heavy smell of scotch drifted from Elle's pod. She tilted her head and squinted "Dannniel??"

Simeon snapped at him. "What do *you* want? My data feed says the wave hasn't even hit yet!"

Daniel drummed his fingers for a second and then stared at Simeon. "I'm leaving. Mind the fort."

"What?!"

Daniel turned to leave and heard both pods latch shut. He ran to the stairs and hollered up, "Chip, let's go!"

From below, Millie had climbed to the Deck 2 stairs and shouted over the motors, "Plasma hits in 20 minutes! I leave in five!" She saw him at the top of the stairs. "Get down here!"

Chip shouted from upstairs that he was right behind.

Daniel followed Millie back to the docking port where she ordered him to climb in, buckle up, and stay quiet. He heard Chip's labored steps down the Deck 2 stairs, so he climbed into the jet and to his usual seat but didn't buckle up in case Chip needed help. Millie climbed in after him and prepared to undock.

The ship began to drifted sideways, which caused Millie and Daniel to lean left as they looked around, confused. Then Daniel realized that Chip must have stopped off on Deck 2 to restore the alignment. He updated Millie: "Just a rotation to keep the habitat in the northern hemisphere." Millie nodded and returned to her preparations.

A moment later, Chip arrived at the hatch and handed down a rectangular leather case. Millie took it and Chip instructed her to give it to Daniel. She handed it back and scolded Daniel for not being buckled up yet. The case slid in front of his knees.

Fortunately, the jet's hatch was sized to transfer payload, as well as people. As Daniel saw Chip climb into the jet, he breathed a sigh of relief and fastened the buckles. Millie was shocked at the size of the passenger. "I only have one seat for you, bud. I hope the straps are long enough."

"Charmed to meet you, as well, madam." Chip wedged into the seat across the aisle from Daniel. Straps and buckles were immaterial.

Millie turned back to Daniel. "That's it? You said four." Chip also looked at him.

"That's it. The others decided to stay in their pods... to watch the fort."

The last phrase brought a grin to Chip, who politely clapped. "Well played, Dan."

Millie pushed the hatch shut, buckled up, and pulled the ceiling latches to release the jet. It fell; Daniel felt nauseous but wasn't alone this time as Chip groaned. Then the engines pitched horizontal and Millie turned on the afterburners, which pressed the passengers into their seats. The twilight widened ahead, and the dashboard message blinked, "Plasma Impact: Imminent."

Millie pointed to a rear facing camera. Between two jet contrails, the sun slipped below the horizon which came alive with a fringe of aurora. "We made it, folks!"

Chip and Daniel cheered and exchanged high fives.

Millie continued, "Make yourselves comfortable. It's a couple of hours to the Northern Depot. Oh, and barf bags are under the seats."

Daniel could finally relax. He lifted the leather case and pulled the zipper down far enough to peek inside. Sunflowers. He closed the zipper and turned to Chip, who watched. "Thank you, Chip."

"Thank *you*." Chip held a piece of paper. "I got a masterpiece, too." He turned it to show Daniel: A colored pencil sketch of a bouquet, surrounded by fallen petals. Daniel felt touched like he hadn't in years.

Chip twisted to face Daniel, as best as the seat and his bulk would permit. His face turned contemplative. "Dan, for the last six years I floated in Paradise. That sounds lovelier than it is. After all, what do I have to show for it? I got fat, played a lot of games, built enough card houses for a city." He chuckled, then shook his head. "And I spent way too much time with a couple of bastards... for sick entertainment." He took a breath and declared, "Those two will ride out this plasma wave just fine. You probably noticed that I reversed our sundial change. But when they exit those pods, they exit my life. I'm sick of being with sick people."

Daniel nodded. "I'll tell ya, I could live a long, happy life and never see them again."

"Funny you put it like that. Today, working with you, I felt a zest for life that I hadn't experienced since, well, since the early ExWhy days." He got a faraway look in his eyes. "We were a team back then, with a vision." He looked back at Daniel, "And I felt that spark again today for the first time in so many years. And it wasn't because it was a life and death situation; no, it took me back to how comradery, how a team, can make the impossible happen. Look at how you acted and how the others did." He bit his lip to fight back emotions.

Daniel hung onto the words.

"Dan, I am done floating. I want a direction, I want a new venture, and I want you to join. I don't even know what it will be, but we'll figure it out." He extended a hand to shake. "Will you join me?"

Daniel's thoughts raced as fast as the jet that cut through the Venusian night. He took Chip's hand. "Of course."

AUTHOR BIO

Brad Ashmore has been an engineer, writer, and inventor of several patents... not necessarily in that order. His writing influences draw from both sci-fi and the absurd. Brad has two children and lives in Silicon Valley with his wife and a bad cat.

When he is not at "Shut Up & Write" Meetups, he can be found in coffee shops writing or working on his next gadget.

Brad also can be found at "UnexpectedBooks.com".

Made in the USA
San Bernardino, CA
07 December 2019

61062938R00073